"If I am to understand correctly," Lord Romford was saying in a cold, clipped voice, "you went to a rout without your chaperone and, because Viscount Brynmawr removed your mask whilst in the middle of the dance floor . . ."

"You make it sound far worse than it was, Hugo," she said quickly. "Honestly, my mask was off only for a fleeting second."

"Long enough for at least three prominent dowagers to recognize you and cause you to remark that as Brynmawr was your fiancé, you were at a loss to understand why anyone should be shocked at your behavior."

"Those women have asp's tongues." Miranda retorted angrily. "I know what I said, but I didn't mean it."

"Whether you meant it or not, my dear, Brynmawr is accepting the situation. He is telling anyone who will listen of the upcoming nuptials and I don't think I'll interfere. Maybe, this time, I will let your behavior stand. This marriage might just be the making of you."

Also by Leonora Blythe:

LADY TARA 23534 $1.50

MIRANDA

Leonora Blythe

FAWCETT COVENTRY ● NEW YORK

For SJEPATJ and J

MIRANDA

Published by Fawcett Coventry Books, a unit of CBS Publications, the Consumer Publishing Division of CBS Inc.

ISBN: 0-449-50048-9

Printed in the United States of America

First Fawcett Coventry Printings: May 1980

10 9 8 7 6 5 4 3 2 1

One

The coach turned into Belgrave Square and the footman prepared to jump down. As it stopped outside number ten, he leapt to the ground and opened the door quickly. With an agility born of experience, he lowered the steps and waited for the occupant to descend. Then, with equal agility, he darted for the door knocker and by the time Lord Romford arrived on the top step, the massive oak portals had been flung open and three lackeys were waiting to receive him.

"My Lord Romford," the footman intoned, "to see Miss Haverfield."

"You are expected, my lord," one of the lackeys said, quickly relieving Lord Romford of his hat, gloves and cane. "Please step this way."

With a scowl deeply ingrained on his face, Lord Romford followed the servant through the main hall, past the large drawing room to the library.

Still frowning, he walked in, dismissing the servant with an impatient gesture. Sitting at the far end of the room, almost hidden behind a pile of papers, was Miss Miranda Haverfield. She wore a worried expression, but when she saw who entered she sprang from her seat and ran to greet her visitor with a smile. This, however, faded as she noticed his reproving look.

"Hugo, I knew you would come," she said tremulously. His apparent ill humor made her uneasy. "Thank you for being so prompt."

Lord Romford's frown deepened as she spoke. Her large eyes, framed by long lashes and her delicate, heart-shaped face were appealing and she had a frailty that made it difficult to be excessively out of sorts with her for long. At least, people who didn't know her well found it so. However, he knew better and this time was determined not to be taken in. Her frailty was no more than a coating, for underneath she had a strength that made her extremely stubborn on occasion.

"Dammit! Miranda," he said finally, "you have the uncanny knack of always getting yourself into trouble when I can give you the least amount of help. I am on my way to Southampton and have but a day to spend here!"

"Please ... please don't look so forbidding, Hugo," she begged in a husky voice. "I know my being your ward imposes a terrible strain on you and, honestly, I do my best to keep out of trouble. Really I do," she added quickly as she saw the look of disbelief cross his face. "This time I am not to blame at all. It was the viscount's fault. If he hadn't insisted on attending the rout in such a disguise, it would never have happened. ... " She broke off with a cry and tapped her feet in agitation. Her

normally brilliant blue eyes were clouded with
tears of frustration. "I don't care how compromised
I am, Hugo, I will *not* marry him."

Much to her surprise, her guardian threw back
his head and laughed, giving her a moment to
survey him without being observed. When he was
not in a bad humor he was a handsome man. His
fair, unpowdered hair, caught at the nape of his
neck by a simple ribbon, accentuated his hooded
eyes and straight nose. They were classic Romford
features. As were his mouth and square jaw. He
stood over six feet in his stocking feet, but, today,
with his heeled boots, he towered above her, making her feel even smaller than her five feet. He was
a careless dresser, yet his clothes fit him snugly
thanks to the efforts of his tailor, and showed off
to perfection his broad shoulders and narrow hips.

"Miranda, Miranda, what am I to do with you?"
he asked, shaking his head. "Last month your horse
bolted down Bond Street. Three months ago I was
just in time to prevent Freddie and Calvin from
fighting a duel over you. Now, it seems, Viscount
Brynmawr is your fiancé. I shudder to think what
else will happen to you. Ring for some refreshment,
there's a good girl, and then let me hear your story
from the beginning."

"I'm sorry, Hugo," she said, moving to the
bellrope. "I forgot you would be thirsty." Encouraged by his change of humor, she gladly obeyed
his command. The interview was going much better
than she had dared hope and if she could scrape
through the next fifteen minutes without quarreling
with him, then, maybe, he would excuse her behavior of last night.

Lord Romford sat down and crossed his legs
casually. Turning his head toward the fire, he

stared thoughtfully at the dancing flames. His ward's hoydenish ways were extremely vexing, and he was at a loss to know what to do to keep her in check. He had assumed guardianship of her nine months ago on the death of her brother. Now, he was close to admitting to himself that perhaps he had made a mistake in agreeing to so mad a scheme. Had he been married, it would have been easy to leave everything to his wife, but he wasn't and he had no idea how to cope with a headstrong young lady of eighteen years. But he hadn't thought to the difficulties ahead when Justin, his closest friend and confidant, had died after a long and painful illness. He had simply given Justin his word that he would undertake to manage Miranda's vast inheritance and ensure that she had some fun before she shackled herself to some worthy whelp. She was beautiful and rich, a combination that could only lead to disaster.

The door opened and a footman appeared, interrupting his reverie.

"You rang, my lady?" he asked.

"Yes, Johnson. Please bring in some refreshments immediately, and . . . and if Mrs. Branley inquires after me, say I am busy in the library. I don't want to be disturbed."

"Very well, my lady," Johnson responded. "Although Mrs. Branley has already asked after you and I said I rather thought you had gone to the Pantheon with Molly and were not expected back until noon."

"What a treasure you are, Johnson. Thank you."

As the door closed behind him, Miranda turned to Lord Romford and saw that he was frowning again.

"Please don't scowl so, Hugo," she begged.

"Johnson has been with our family for years and knows exactly what I want him to say. Mrs. Branley might well be your cousin, but she certainly doesn't have your fine understanding."

"Understanding nothing, Miranda," Lord Romford said sharply, disturbed by yet another example of her unconventional manners. "Mrs. Branley is your chaperone and that you should have cozened the footman into lying about your movements is appalling. I have a good mind to summon her here now, and have her tell me exactly what happened at the rout."

"Please don't," she said in a small voice. "You see, the whole trouble arose because she wasn't with me." She broke off as she saw the look of outrage spread across her guardian's face, but pride came to her rescue. Her chin went up and her gaze didn't waver under his harsh scrutiny.

They were standing thus when Johnson returned with a laden tray, which he quickly put down, and withdrew.

"I don't give too much on hers getting out of this one lightly," he remarked to the underfootman. "It looks like real trouble abrewing in there."

"If I am to understand correctly," Lord Romford was saying in a cold, clipped voice, "you went to a rout in Vauxhall without your chaperone and because Viscount Brynmawr removed your mask whilst in the middle of the dance floor . . ." He paused for a moment to look at Miranda for confirmation of these facts.

"You make it sound far worse than it was, Hugo," she said quickly. "Honestly, my mask was off only for a fleeting second." Even as she spoke she was wondering how he had discovered so much so quickly.

"Long enough for at least three prominent dowagers to recognize you and cause enough of a commotion to force you to remark to Mrs. Jeffries that as Brynmawr was your fiancé, you were at a loss to understand why anyone should be shocked by your behavior."

"That woman has an asp's tongue," Miranda retorted angrily. "I know what I said, but I didn't mean it."

"Whether you meant it or not, my dear, Brynmawr is accepting the situation. I left him not ten minutes ago at White's and he was busy repeating plans for the upcoming nuptials to anyone who would listen."

"I cannot believe it," Miranda whispered in despair. "You must tell him that it isn't so, Hugo, for it is obvious he won't listen to me."

Hugo shook his head slowly. "No, Miranda, I don't think I'll interfere. Maybe, this time, I'll let things stand. This marriage might just be the making of you. God knows, I have tried to be patient with you. I know Mrs. Branley has done her best to keep you in check. Who knows, Viscount Brynmawr may succeed where we have failed."

"Hugo, please listen," Miranda pleaded, desperately biting back her tears. "You cannot allow such a marriage. Why, he is not only old enough to be my father, but I loathe him."

"My mind is made up," Lord Romford said. "I will send the announcement to *The Times* today. We can proceed with the wedding arrangements when I return. And, my dear ward, for your edification, the viscount is but two years my senior and I have never considered myself old enough to be your father."

She burst into tears and cracked her fan against

the arm of a chair. "I won't do it, Hugo," she stormed. "I don't care what you say."

He looked at her sternly. "Enough of your hysterics, Miranda," he commanded impatiently. "My mind is set. I have arranged for you to go to Ramsden until all the brouhaha from last night has died down." He looked at her sitting there so forlornly and experienced a moment of remorse. She really was a dear child. It was a great pity she had no family to protect her from herself. Maybe he was being too hard. Somehow it seemed criminal to force her into a marriage she found distasteful; it was tantamount to caging a wild bird. Yet, he was not unhopeful that the viscount would be just the right sort of husband for her. He was patient, gentle and, though not overly plump in the pocket, had enough money to live comfortably, and, the most important factor, had been unashamedly infatuated with Miranda for the longest time. With a sudden resolve to do the best for his ward, he decided to soften his stand. "Do you really loathe him?" he asked abruptly.

Miranda turned her tear-stained face toward her guardian. A faint hope that he would relent lit her eyes. "Well . . . no, Hugo," she admitted reluctantly. "But . . . but, I don't feel I could ever love him enough to want to marry him."

"Yet you were prepared to let people think so last night," Lord Romford remarked dryly. "No, not again," he said quickly as he saw the tears spring into her eyes. "I fully intend to send you to Ramsden, but I will hold off sending out the betrothal announcements. I will suggest to Brynmawr that he repair to his estates, which, as you know, abut mine, to give you time to get better acquainted"—he paused to allow Miranda to absorb this slight adjustment to his plan—"and, when I return from Southampton, we can think about making the necessary arrangements."

Miranda, realizing from the stubborn set to his jaw that he meant what he said, sighed unhappily. "I have to agree, don't I?" she said miserably. "I won't change my mind, though, about Rodney. In fact," she continued quickly, "I shall probably turn into a shrew with boredom, especially if I only have Mrs. Branley to converse with, and that might make Rodney dread the fact that I will become his wife."

"I have thought of that, my dear," Lord Romford responded, smiling in the lopsided way that Miranda usually found irresistible. "I intend to ask Cousin Anita to join you."

"Anita!" Miranda exclaimed. "'Pon rep that is the best thing you have suggested yet, Hugo. Why your other relatives cannot be as lovely is something I will never comprehend."

Her enthusiasm was infectious and Lord Romford found himself laughing at her change in temper. "It is to be hoped that Anita will use her common sense and intelligence to show you the error of your ways, young lady," he said jocularly.

"Oh! No, not Anita," Miranda responded cheerfully. "She might well have donned her spinster cap, but she has by no means lost her sense of humor. Why, only the other day in St. James's Park I saw a particularly fine gentleman surveying her intently through his quizzing glass. And do you know what she said when I drew her attention to this phenomenon?"

Lord Romford shook his head. "I cannot imagine," he murmured.

" 'That, surely, must be Horace Bateman.' And

when I expressed my ignorance of this man she said, 'It is not to be expected that you know him, but his three aging maiden aunts died last year. He had spent a lot of time with them and was very fond of them. Now, it seems, he considers himself an authority on women who have been left on the shelf.' I told her, Hugo, that she was making no sense, but she just laughed. 'Why, dear Miranda, he is collecting material for a book he intends to have published for us poor unfortunates, giving us advice on how best to cope with our lowly status.' "

"It doesn't sound very interesting to me," Lord Romford said.

"Exactly my sentiments," Miranda replied. "Anita, however, was vastly amused because she has heard that he firmly believes spinsters all hanker after a little attention from the opposite sex. Hence, he ogles them whenever he has the chance."

"Anita is still far from reaching that status," Lord Romford said, seemingly surprised by the revelation that his cousin considered herself in that light.

"I told her, but you know Anita," Miranda said. "She says she is very happy looking after her sister's children."

"Be that as it may," Lord Romford said mildly, "we are allowing ourselves to get sidetracked. I shall join you at Ramsden in a sennight and talk with you further about your upcoming nuptials. In the meantime, I beg you not to try Mrs. Branley's patience too much."

Although thankful for the short reprieve her guardian had granted her, Miranda knew that she had lost and did her best to conceal her dismay. "I will do my best to behave with the utmost propriety," she said lightly. "What is more, I will endeavor to keep out of trouble until you return."

"I would hope so," he replied shortly, "for I'm sure Anita would be none too pleased if she had to cope with an attack of Mrs. Branley's vapors that your hoydenish ways inevitably bring about."

"That's unfair, Hugo," she said hotly, for the truth of his words made her angry. "She only indulges in those attacks because she enjoys the attention they bring."

"That is quite enough, Miranda. I will not tolerate such impudence. You must learn to curb your tongue before you land yourself in deep trouble."

"I . . . I can't believe that you mean to be so unfeeling," Miranda managed. "You act as though you have never been young, or ever kicked up your heels for a lark. But I know from Justin that that simply isn't so."

Doing his best to ignore her outburst, Lord Romford rose from his chair. There seemed to be no way to explain to his ward that there was a world of difference between two young men sowing their wild oats and a young lady acting foolishly. At least, no way that wouldn't embroil them in another heated dispute. "I refuse to be drawn into any further discussion on that topic, Miranda," he said in tones that brooked no argument. "I have said all that is necessary. I trust that you will see the error of your ways and do your best to mend them."

He bowed perfunctorily and left. Miranda stared stormily at her guardian's retreating figure. It was always the same, she thought miserably. They simply couldn't be together without fighting.

Lord Romford's temper subsided the moment he left the room. For a second he was tempted to return and smooth things over, but he dismissed the idea quickly. Miranda would have to learn to be more circumspect in the future, and if expressing his disapproval at her more outrageous behavior helped, then it was surely best to leave things the way they were. Instead, he stopped in briefly to see Mrs. Branley, who was in her sitting room. He wanted to ensure that this worthy lady knew that while she was to keep a discreet eye on the couple, she was to do her utmost to promote the match.

"And don't make too much of last night, Clarissa," he cautioned. "Miranda is filled with remorse and knows that she overstepped the mark."

With a birdlike motion, Mrs. Branley dabbed her eyes with a delicate lace handkerchief as she nodded her assent. She felt unequal to the task of telling her awe-inspiring cousin that she had long since given up trying to control his wayward charge.

Lord Romford was thoughtful as he rode away. It was difficult to know whether or not he was doing the right thing. There was no doubt that his life had taken a strange turn since Justin's death. For to assume the responsibility of a young lady scarce out of the schoolroom had caused many complications. He had neither been prepared for them, nor the gossip, some malicious, that followed. Everyone he knew, it seemed, tried to link his name with Miranda's. The only thing he could be thankful for was that Miranda was too young to realize the implications of such talk. Maybe this marriage would silence those clacking tongues and she would be allowed to lead a normal life. That, in turn, would allow him to resume his old pursuits and hobbies.

This prospect, which should have cheered him considerably, left him feeling sadly flat. However, he was able to put this down to the fact that the last nine months had been very trying. It would probably take him a little time to realize he was free. Free to do as he wished without having to worry what anyone would say.

Two

Ramsden, a minor estate of Lord Romford's, was situated in the village of Tintern in the Wye Valley of Wales. The surrounding scenery was wild and beautiful, and the pine forests that rose steeply from the banks of the river held an air of secrecy. The Wye snaked down the valley majestically and was a favored spot for all serious fishermen. Lord Romford had spent many hours in his youth standing on the banks, casting his lines into the cold winter waters, hoping to land a salmon or an umber. Indeed, one had to be a determined fisherman, for the winter was the season for these fish and a Welsh winter was usually marked by heavy rains.

The mountains around were dotted with hafods, the summer huts of the farm workers. Lord Romford, his brother Felix and Justin had often spent nights in these dwellings. For food they would eat the dried oatcakes that were usually stored there, and drink the water from the natural springs that were to be found in abundance.

Miranda knew this from her brother. She sighed unhappily. Justin's death was still painful to her. She missed him tremendously. If he were still alive she wouldn't be in such a predicament now. *Why, oh, why had she promised him she would accept Hugo as her guardian?* She should have realized that under his seemingly carefree manner Hugo was an overbearing and odious person with absolutely no understanding of the female sex. The very fact that he was still a bachelor was proof of this.

She glanced at her traveling companions and allowed another sigh to escape. Mrs. Branley, bundled up against the elements, as she was so fond of saying, was almost unrecognizable, hidden as she was under a voluminous cloak and muffler. One would think it winter, not summer, to judge by her dress. Anita, on the other hand, was wearing more appropriate clothes for the time of year. A red dress of heavy cotton with a matching light wool shawl draped over her shoulders.

Conversation since they had left the posting house at Reading had been desultory. Mrs. Branley, after complaining that the noise in the taproom directly beneath her room had kept her awake all night, had lapsed into a fitful doze and Anita was deep in a book.

"We're lucky it's not raining," Miranda observed.

Anita looked up and smiled absentmindedly. "According to this almanac I'm reading, it forecasts a dry summer. I hope it will be so, for Ramsden always shows its best face in the sunshine." She was looking forward to her stay, for, like her cousin

Lord Romford, she loved Ramsden and hadn't visited it in many years.

The house was considered simple by modern standards, although, with its eight bedrooms, a large library, a gallery which housed the Romford art collection, and the several drawing rooms, Anita considered it a rather grand residence. There were even secret passageways and concealed priest holes, but Lord Romford's father had had these blocked up.

The long driveway was lined with dozens of mountain ash which gave good protection from the easterly winds that swept across from the Bristol Channel. Now, as the coach rolled to a halt at the main entrance, Anita sighed happily. "How thoughtful of Hugo to ask me to stay," she remarked. "I hadn't realized until now how much I have missed the country."

"The air is certainly invigorating," Miranda replied, suppressing a yawn. "Is that not so, Mrs. Branley?" she asked of her elderly companion.

"Oh! Dearie me, I don't know, child," Mrs. Branley said, opening her eyes. "I can only hope that Hugo had the foresight to send advance warning of our arrival so that all the beds will have been aired and fires lit." She put a small handkerchief to her nose just in time to catch a sneeze. "I knew it," she muttered triumphantly. "I have caught cold."

"Mrs. Lloyd will take care of you," Anita said quickly. "She is full of remedies for all ailments." Mrs. Lloyd was the permanent housekeeper at Ramsden.

Two liveried footmen had opened the coach doors by this time, and pulled down the steps. Now they waited patiently for the occupants to descend.

Miranda jumped down first and looked at the house she had heard so much about but never seen. The facade was the epitome of simplicity, gray stones covered by creepers. The wide bow windows, looking out on the rolling countryside, were the only relief the stark north side of the manor sported. Offsetting this severity on the west side were two ornate arches that allowed glimpses of the rose garden beyond. Tall chimneys rose from the slate roofs and smoke spiraled lazily toward the cloudy sky from them all. For once the wind wasn't blowing.

Miranda turned as Mrs. Branley joined her. "I think we are expected," she said as she moved toward the front steps. She was about to put her dainty foot on the first one when the front doors opened and three dogs rushed down, almost knocking themselves and her over in their enthusiastic greeting. It took a few minutes to untangle herself, by which time she found herself being kissed heartily on the cheek by a young man with a cheerful countenance. His tousled hair and muddied boots indicated that he had spent much of the morning outdoors.

"Felix," she gasped in surprise. "What on earth are you doing here?"

"A question I would have asked had I seen you first," Anita interrupted. "Does Hugo know you're here?" she inquired as she watched Miranda untie her bonnet strings and straighten this becoming confection that Felix had pushed sideways.

"What! Tell my brother I've been sent down, coz?" he exclaimed in horror. "Hardly. I thought to be safe here, but to be invaded by two of the prettiest ladies I know is the luckiest thing that has happened to me in an age."

The three young people were brought up short as Mrs. Branley was seized with another bout of sneezing. "Take me inside, quickly, before I catch my death," she moaned. "I must retire to my bedchamber immediately."

Felix gallantly gave her his arm and led the way. As she passed Anita she whispered, "I'm so sorry to abandon you, my dear, but you do understand, don't you?" Her tone was apologetic, but Anita discerned a look of great relief in her eyes.

She laughed ruefully. "Of course I do, Clarissa."

The few servants that were in residence stood in two lines in the front hall, forming a narrow path for the visitors. They bowed and curtsied to show their respect and Mrs. Lloyd stepped forward to greet the guests. Anita explained Mrs. Branley's plight and without more ado Mrs. Lloyd took the elderly chaperone in hand, ordering a maid to bring hot bricks to the yellow bedroom immediately.

"When I heard you were to be among the party, Mrs. Branley," she said, "I remembered that you particularly liked that room the last time you were here."

"How very thoughtful of you, Mrs. Lloyd," Mrs. Branley replied. The rest of her words were lost to the people in the hallway as the two women rounded the bend in the stairs and disappeared from view.

For the first time since her interview with Lord Romford, Miranda felt happy. She giggled and gleefully clapped her hands. "I have spent the last two days dreading this enforced rustication," she said, "but suddenly all is well. I know I shall have a famous time now that Mrs. Branley is indisposed. . . ."

". . . But I will be close on your heels to remind

you of the reason we are here," Anita said severely, sweeping Felix and Miranda into the sitting room, away from the gaping stares of the servants. She closed the door firmly. "As for you, Felix, you must give me your word that you will not encourage Miranda to make a cake of herself. We don't want the locals gossiping, especially since she will probably be spending a lot more time here once the marriage has taken place."

It was Felix's turn to look surprised. "Marriage? By all that's wonderful," he exclaimed. "And I had thought your heart was mine." He paused dramatically to put his hand on his chest. "Who is this cad that dares usurp my place?"

Miranda cast a despairing look at Anita, for Felix's light banter brought her back to reality and served to underline the uncomfortable position she was now in. "'Tis not a love match," she said in a subdued voice, "but one that Hugo thinks will be the making of me."

"Come, Miranda," Anita said briskly. "I hear that Viscount Brynmawr is a charming, intelligent man, and I'm sure you will deal well together."

Felix interrupted this with a low whistle. "Our most worthy neighbor," he said and was about to make another observation when he realized that Miranda was having difficulty in maintaining her composure. "Well, now, why don't you tell me what this is all about? I cannot believe that my brother would force you into a marriage you find distasteful." He frowned as he spoke, the resemblance to his brother becoming marked.

"It is because of my own foolishness," Miranda responded with characteristic honesty. "And . . . and now, it seems, I must pay the price."

Felix looked to Anita for clarification of this statement.

"I can only give it to you third hand," she said in response to his raised eyebrows. "As far as I can comprehend, Miranda got the notion to go to a Vauxhall rout, unescorted."

"I *was* wearing a mask," Miranda filled in. "And nobody recognized me."

"Until the viscount removed it. . . ."

"Why on earth did you permit such a thing, you silly peagoose?" Felix asked in astonishment.

"I dared him to," Miranda said defiantly. "He thought I was the little girl who danced third from the right in the chorus line at Covent Garden and . . ."

". . . you replied, 'If that is what you really believe, my lord, expose me,' " Felix finished for her.

"Something to that effect," Miranda confirmed sheepishly. "But I swear I only spoke so because of the insult he had delivered. I never thought he would do such a thing."

"Must have been in his cups," Felix observed sagely. "For, in general, he is the most mild-mannered person."

Anita, seeing that a continuation of this conversation would only serve to further upset her charge, deftly changed the topic. "Would it appear too inquisitive of me if I were to inquire what necessitated your removal from Oxford, Felix?" she asked in dulcet tones.

"Nothing of any import," he replied airily. "Old Babbington took exception to my bringing a parrot into his lecture on some Greek poet."

"I fail to see why he should object," Miranda said

judicially. "He could hardly expect you to keep it locked in your rooms."

"Quite so," Felix agreed, pleased by such understanding. "And, I think the entire episode would have escaped the old man's attention except that Sidney, that's the parrot, shouted out 'Silly old fool' just as Babbington was coming to his summation."

"Most provoking," Anita remarked in mellifluous accents.

"Odiously so," Felix said earnestly. "I was, of course, dismissed immediately and never given the chance to explain how it all came about."

"No doubt Hugo will understand," was all Anita said, knowing full well that he wouldn't. "You can tell him all about it when he joins us."

"What, Hugo is arriving as well?" he said a little nervously. "When?"

"Not for a sennight," Miranda reassured him. "It gives us plenty of time to think up an excuse for your presence here. So please don't worry on that score, for I swear I will need all your attention to help divert me from my problems. Rodney arrives in a day or so and will begin his courtship in earnest. Oh, Felix," she said miserably, "what on earth can I do to persuade him that we will not suit?"

"Miranda!" Anita's shocked voice cut in. "I will not stand by and listen to such nonsense. And, as for you, Felix," she continued, turning to face Felix squarely, "if you do anything, and I mean anything, to overset the arrangements, I shall write to Hugo *immediately.*"

"That's blackmail, coz," he protested with a laugh. "I refuse to believe that you are capable of being so mean-spirited."

"Don't try my patience too far, then, Felix," she

responded as she walked gracefully to the door, "for I don't want to disillusion you. I'm not saying that you can't enjoy yourselves. Just don't do anything that will jeopardize Miranda's engagement." She left the room and closed the door gently behind her. She couldn't have issued a clearer warning, yet she was filled with misgivings. Felix, an irrepressible, though lovable, scamp was totally incapable of keeping out of mischief. And Miranda was never in need of much encouragement to follow suit. She sighed unhappily. Mrs. Branley would undoubtedly use her cold as an excuse to keep to her room, leaving her to cope with the situation alone.

Three

Four days had passed since they had arrived at Ramsden and still there was no sign that Mrs. Branley was ready to leave her room. In fact, she had just sent word to Anita, through the housekeeper, that her cold had worsened. However, this particular morning, Anita was more concerned for her own peace of mind than Mrs. Branley's health.

All her forebodings were coming true and she was in a quandary about what to do next. Twice, now, she had discovered Miranda dressed in Felix's clothes, roaming the countryside at will. When she had pointed out to Miranda how unseemly her behavior was, Miranda had been quick to reply that when Justin was alive he had never objected. It was much easier, she had continued, to enjoy oneself dressed in such a style, for it meant that she didn't have to worry about dirtying or tearing her muslins. Anyway, she wanted to keep them fresh for the arrival of the viscount.

Anita sighed as she adjusted her cap. In all her four and twenty years she had never felt so torn. Her loyalty should be toward her cousin, yet Miranda was so obviously unhappy about her forthcoming marriage it was impossible to be too harsh on the child and put an end to her enjoyment. She dreaded to think what Romford would say if he found out, then dismissed the thought, deciding practically that she couldn't waste her time worrying over something that might not happen.

As she put the finishing touches to her toilet, she glanced at herself in the gilt-framed mirror that adorned her dressing table. She smiled ruefully at her image. Her sister had always said that with more careful grooming her countenance could be considered pleasing. Well, she neither had the time, nor the inclination, to spend hours pampering herself. In general, she was satisfied with the way she looked. She was tall, some thought too tall, and slender. Her large gray eyes were framed by dark lashes and her cheeks were pink and glowed with health.

"A perfect candidate for Mr. Horace Bateman," she murmured to herself.

"What nonsense," Miranda said with a laugh. "I swear that if you do away with your caps, Anita, you would have difficulty fighting off suitors."

Anita whirled around, a becoming blush flooding her cheeks. She was embarrassed to have been caught in such a position. "h! Miranda!" she exclaimed. "You frightened me. I didn't even hear you enter."

"I did knock," Miranda replied with a grin, "but you didn't hear." She flung herself down, in a most unladylike fashion, on a chaise that nestled in the window recess, her lips pulled down in an unbecoming pout. "Rodney arrives tomorrow," she announced miserably. "Whatever am I going to do?"

"Start behaving like the lady you are supposed to be," Anita said practically, but her sympathetic smile took the sting out of her words. "Seriously, Miranda," she continued earnestly, "you must give yourself time to get to know Viscount Brynmawr. I have never met him, but I hear he is a charming man."

"But you don't understand, Anita," Miranda replied. "I have known him forever and have always regarded him as a friend of Justin's. He's . . . so . . . so . . . staid."

"Staid?" Anita queried in amazement. "I hardly think that his conduct at the rout can be considered staid."

"I know," Miranda said defensively, "but that's the only time in all the years I've known him that he has behaved in such a manner. Anita, don't you understand? He's too mild for me. I need someone strong, with vitality and . . . and . . . who sees me as I am. Rodney has me on a pedestal and is blinded to my faults. He . . . he thinks I'm perfect."

Anita suppressed a smile with great difficulty at this. "He must love you very much, then," was all she said.

"We shall see," Miranda responded. "Maybe he will realize after he has spent a few days with me that I'm a human being and not an angel."

"I hope you aren't deliberately planning to shock him, Miranda," Anita said quickly.

Miranda smiled wanly. "No. Hugo would never forgive me if I did, and for all that I complain about his high-handed ways, I couldn't bear to have to endure his censure for the rest of my life."

"Well, that's certainly a relief to hear," Anita remarked, pleased that Miranda had decided to act sensibly. "Now, if you'll take a piece of advice from a friend," she continued, "I would suggest you go across the fields and look at Rossfield. It's a pleasant walk and I'm sure you'll like the house."

Miranda pulled a face. "I promised Felix I would go riding with him."

"Felix can wait for once. Do as I suggest, I beg you." She was anxious for Miranda to go because she knew that her charge would be impressed by the grandeur of Rossfield. Also, she felt it a good thing for Miranda to spend some time alone, away from Felix.

"Come with me," Miranda said. "Then, if I'm stopped by Rodney's gamekeeper, I won't feel so foolish."

"Nonsense. You are perfectly capable of taking a stroll by yourself. And it's the most natural thing to want to view the property of which you are about to become mistress. I have a few chores I must accomplish today and I must write to my sister." She walked over to Miranda and helped her up off the chaise. "Go on, my dear," she urged. "I know you will enjoy yourself."

Miranda stood hesitantly for a moment and Anita could sense that she felt reluctant about seeing Rossfield alone.

"I could take the dogs with me, I suppose," she said slowly, "although I do wish you would change your mind."

"Be off with you," Anita chided gently. "A little time for quiet reflection is just what you need."

Miranda again pulled a face. "I've done enough

of that and it hasn't helped. But I'll do as you suggest if it makes you happy, Anita."

Anita merely nodded and watched as Miranda walked slowly from the room.

As Miranda descended the stairs she called for the dogs. The June day was warm and she had no need for her cloak, and they were soon outside in the fresh air. The three dogs sensing freedom, bounded off in different directions and only came to heel when Miranda called to them sharply. They stood looking up at her, their tails wagging and tongues hanging out.

"We're going for a walk," she instructed her canine audience. "You must promise to behave, otherwise Rodney's gamekeeper will be angry." One of the dogs barked as if in response and Miranda laughed. "All right," she said, "as long as you all understand." Stooping down, she picked up a stone and threw it in the direction of Rossfield. "Let us advance, in order, my boys, and see what delights are in store for me." She spoke to herself, however, for the dogs had already gone.

She walked briskly, enjoying the fresh air and warm sun. The dogs chased on ahead but every so often trotted back to make certain she was still there. As she climbed over the last stile on Lord Romford's property, she paused briefly. For the last few days she had deliberately avoided coming in this direction. It was almost as though she had convinced herself that as long as she didn't see Rossfield, it didn't exist.

"Well, now it's time to face the future, my girl," she told herself. "And, unless something drastic happens, you are about to become the Right Honorable, the Viscountess Brynmawr." Tears clouded her vision momentarily, but with characteristic impatience she brushed them away.

Stepping down gingerly from her perch, she proceeded across the field. Her pretty blue muslin was already dirty about the hem. She was heedless of this, though, as she looked ahead to catch the first glimpse of the house. She could already see the towering chimneys and as she passed a clump of trees, the entire mansion suddenly came into view. She stopped and drew in her breath. Anita was right. Rossfield was imposing.

Unlike Ramsden, which had been modernized to the extent of moving the main living rooms to ground level, Rossfield clung to its Elizabethan heritage. It was a tall, wide and shallow house on four floors. The porch protruded to form an impressive front door and on each side a wide bay thrust out. The facade was symmetrical, even to the equal spacing of the rainwater pipes, but somehow the effect was grandiloquent. Time had mellowed the stonework, giving the building a pleasant mottled appearance which compensated for the lack of any creeper growing up the walls. Liking what she saw, Miranda failed to notice that it was in great need of repair.

She moved forward slowly, calling for the dogs as she went. The idea of being mistress to all this splendor was rather appealing, but still she couldn't envision herself the wife of the viscount. By now she had entered the forecourt. The lawns were immaculate and the rose garden, to her left, was beginning to flower. The atmosphere was serene and she found herself relaxing slightly. Taking one last look at the house, she turned and started back toward Ramsden. The dogs, as if sensing her unhappiness, kept close to her. It was as though they were her escort. This, however, lasted only a few minutes, for the sound of a gunshot sent the three of them off.

Startled by the blast, Miranda followed them, and by the time she had caught up with them they were sniffing excitedly in a hedgerow. Thinking a rabbit was the cause of their joy, she called them to heel and pushed past them to investigate. An involuntary gasp of horror escaped her as she saw a man, covered in blood, on the ground. He was alive, but badly wounded. Quickly turning to the dogs, she commanded them to sit. She knelt down and took the man's wrist in her hand. She felt for his pulse. It was weak and rapid. His eyes were closed, his breathing shallow. She hesitated for a moment, then lifted her dress to expose her petticoats. Working rapidly, she started to pull at the frills, until she had managed to tear them free. Then, in the vain hope that she could stem the flow of blood that was coming from the wound in his chest, she pressed the makeshift padding over his thin blue jacket.

The pressure she applied jarred the man into consciousness and he grabbed at her hand.

"It's too late for that, miss," he gasped feebly. "It's too late."

Appalled by his pallor, Miranda drew back. "I don't know what else to do," she responded quietly. "I must go for help."

"Come 'ere," the man commanded weakly. "Just listen to what I have's to say, for there's no saying but that you'll be the last to see me alive." He broke off as he started to cough, but didn't let go of Miranda's hand. "Come closer," he whispered. "I've not much strength left."

Miranda did as he requested, too frightened to

refuse. Never, in all her life, had she been witness to such a scene.

"See this ring on my finger?" Miranda nodded. "Take it off, and keep it safe. Easy now," he said hoarsely, as she tugged it off. "And remember," he continued weakly, "the queen makes the straight flush." The effort of speech proved too much for him and his head fell back onto the earth as he fainted away.

"Sir, sir," Miranda shouted urgently, pulling her hand free. "Wake up. Please wake up."

The man's only response was a long, low, shuddering moan. Miranda stood up and looked around. There was no one in sight. Terrified by what she had witnessed, she pocketed the ring and ran toward Ramsden. The man needed help urgently. The dogs, after one final inspection of the body, followed her and a few minutes later they arrived home. Thankful to be in a safe sanctuary, Miranda ran up the front steps and burst into tears as she saw Felix crossing the main hall on his way to the kitchens.

"Whatever is the matter?" he asked. "You look as though you have been dragged through a hedgerow backward."

Miranda looked down at her bloodied skirts as though bewildered by her appearance. "Felix, quickly," she sobbed. "There's a man dying in the south field. He's been shot."

"A man . . . what?" Felix started to say but stopped as Miranda swayed. He was at her side in a trice and caught her before she fell. He picked her up and carried her into the sitting room and as he laid her down gently on the gold brocade couch, Anita walked in.

"I heard a noise," she said, unable to see what

Felix was doing, for he had his back to her. "Is
something the matter?"

"I'd say," Felix responded manfully, as he
straightened himself up. "Take care of Miranda
while I go and investigate her story. She claims that
a man has been shot in the fields."

"What a coil," Anita remarked distractedly.
"Hugo will never believe Miranda was there by
accident. Now that's a silly thing to say," she
continued. "The poor child has received a fearsome
shock and I can only think of what her guardian's
reaction will be."

Felix was staring at her in astonishment. He had
never seen his cousin so flustered. "Are you sure you
can manage by yourself, Cousin Anita?" he asked.
"Do you want me to send for Mrs. Lloyd?"

"No, no. I'm perfectly all right. It was just the
sight of all that blood. I . . . I thought it was
Miranda's at first. It's all my fault, I urged her to
go to Rossfield, completely forgetting the gamekeeper's warning that he had spotted a man loiter-
ing near the house on several occasions recently."

"I'll take Jake with me, in that case," Felix said,
referring to the gamekeeper, "just in case anything
untoward happens." With that he left the room.

Left alone, Anita forced herself to calm down.
She tucked a throw rug about Miranda and felt for
her pulse. There was nothing more she could do
until Miranda regained consciousness, except inform Lord Romford. She sat down and penned a
note to him, requesting him to join the party at
Ramsden as quickly as possible.

Four

Lord Romford sat at ease in his private room at the Green Anchor. He had spent a satisfying few days overseeing the repairs to his ketch, *The Tawny Owl,* and was now contemplating the pleasures ahead of him. He was expecting his mistress, Henrietta, to arrive that evening to spend a few days with him before he joined his ward at Ramsden. It would be good to see Henrietta again, and he found himself looking forward to her arrival.

Henrietta Devlin was an extremely attractive widow and he had been discreetly enjoying her company for the past two months. She had agreed to see him in Southampton, for, as she had said last week, she had to break her journey to Cornwall somewhere and Southampton was as good a place as any. There was no pretense of love between them and no talk of marriage. So, while Lord Romford realized that she would eventually leave him to marry one of her many suitors, he was content to enjoy their relationship for as long as it lasted.

A discreet knock at the door interrupted his thoughts and he bade the visitor enter. Looking up, he saw it was the captain of *The Owl.* "Everything under control, Captain Jones?" he asked warmly. He admired this taciturn man's ability immensely.

"Aye, m'lord," Captain Jones responded in a gruff voice, his weatherbeaten face expressionless. "I just came to report that the topsail and boom will be here by the end of the week and we should be seaworthy in ten days."

"In that case, you had best bring *The Owl* round to Newport when all is ready and send word to me at Ramsden when you arrive." His voice expressed the disappointment he felt. He had been hoping to make the trip himself, but he couldn't afford to wait another ten days. There was no telling what Miranda could get up to in that length of time.

Captain Jones nodded. "Very good, m'lord. I'm sorry it's going to take so long, for it would have been nice to have you aboard again."

Lord Romford gave a rueful chuckle. "Never mind, Captain. We'll make up for it one day. By the way," he continued, "what do you know of that boy I met today on the quayside? Tim, I believe he said his name was. I hear he's looking for a boat to join."

The captain's face broke into a sudden smile. "I'd like to have him aboard, m'lord," he replied enthusiastically. "Tim's a capable little monkey and not an ounce of fear in his whole body. He could be very useful, especially as we're a bit short handed since Ross left."

"Then hire him and pay what he's worth," Lord Romford said promptly. "I think he'll make a damned fine sailor one day."

"No doubt about it," Captain Jones concurred. "I'll go and talk to the lad's father tomorrow and start Tim right away."

"Good. It's settled then. If, perchance, Tim's father objects, let me know and I'll talk to him."

"I can't see as how he would, m'lord. In fact, I happen to know he'll be glad to let the lad go, him being a widower with six other children to provide for."

Lord Romford smiled. Captain Jones's knowledge of the local families never failed to amaze him. It always seemed that he knew everyone who lived within a five-mile radius of any port he visited.

"I'd best be getting back now, m'lord," the captain continued. "There's no telling what mischief has taken place in my absence." He gave a perfunctory bow and left.

Lord Romford rose from his chair and moved to the long windows. His rooms, on the second floor of the inn, overlooked the harbor, a view he never tired of. He watched Captain Jones walk down the narrow cobblestoned street, until the sudden movement of somebody darting out of a shop doorway after the captain caught his eye. He smiled as he recognized the young boy, Tim. His smile turned to laughter as he saw Captain Jones turn and greet the boy with a slow nod of his head.

"So that was what the good captain really wanted," he murmured, and for some reason felt inordinately pleased that he had been the one to mention Tim first.

His thoughts then turned to his ward. He wondered if she was happier about her engagement now than she had been when he had last seen her. He wished for the thousandth time that he understood her as well as he did the captain. Life would be much easier for them both. In an effort to shake these thoughts, he turned back into the room and paused in front of the mirror. He looked at himself for a moment, straightened his cravat and moved away. His earlier mood of tranquility had vanished; now he felt restless. It was always the same when he thought about Miranda. Well, Henrietta should help dispel the feeling, and, with luck, she would be here in time for dinner.

The sounds of a carriage pulling up in the courtyard sent him back to the window. It would be a pleasant surprise if it were Henrietta arriving early. However, when he saw the hired chaise, he shrugged his shoulders in disappointment. It most certainly wasn't Henrietta, for she would never travel in such a dowdy conveyance. Further disappointment was in store, when Watkins, his valet, appeared bearing a heavily scented note on a silver tray.

"A messenger has just arrived with this, m'lord," he intoned gravely.

Lord Romford recognized the bold handwriting immediately. He opened the letter and quickly read the few lines. He reread it slowly and let out an oath. It was from Henrietta, letting him know she wouldn't be coming. He knew of her long-standing friendship with Sir Frampton-Wallace, she wrote, so it should come as no surprise to him to hear that Sir Frampton-Wallace had finally asked her to marry him. She was sorry to end their relationship so abruptly, and hoped he would understand and forgive her.

He turned to Watkins with a frown. "Insure that the messenger is fed before he returns to London," he ordered, "and then pack my things. We will leave for Ramsden immediately."

"Very good, m'lord," Watkins replied impassively. "I'll see to it right away."

As soon as he was alone, Lord Romford tore up the letter. "I wish you luck, Henrietta," he said softly. He was genuinely pleased for her, and knew that Sir Frampton-Wallace, who was considerably older than Henrietta, would allow her the freedom she needed.

Two days later, when he turned into the long driveway at Ramsden he knew immediately that something was wrong. A strange carriage was standing outside the house and a portly gentleman was just alighting. Curious to know what had happened, he urged his horse to a gallop and covered the last hundred yards quickly. Relinquishing the reins to a groom who had scurried from the stables at his approach, he made his way into the house. The first person he saw was Felix and once over the momentary astonishment at seeing his brother, he greeted him warily.

"Hello, Hugo," Felix replied sheepishly. "Didn't expect to see you for a few days. But it's a good thing you got here quickly, for you're in time for the inquest."

"Inquest?" Lord Romford queried, a worried frown creasing his brow. "What, in heaven's name, has happened?"

"What!" Felix exclaimed, "You haven't received Anita's note? We'd best go to your study so that I can explain things."

Lord Romford nodded. His brother's manner told him that the dead person wasn't a close member of the family, so he was content to wait until they were safely ensconced in the study, their privacy ensured, before demanding an explanation.

Briefly, Felix told him of Miranda's discovery, and the man's subsequent death. "The squire suggested to Dr. Thompson, he's been appointed coroner, that the inquest be held here. Better for Miranda, he said. In fact the doctor has just arrived and I was on my way to greet him."

"He can wait a little longer," Lord Romford said, perturbed by the news. "I have a few more questions. How is Miranda? Is she in a state of shock?"

Felix laughed. "Not Miranda. She was a bit upset to begin with, but she really doesn't remember much of what happened. Her real concern is how you will react."

"Why on earth would that worry her?" Lord Romford asked in amazement.

"Lord only knows. Said something about you being bound to think it her fault."

"That's absolutely absurd. Send her to me immediately and we'll clear up that piece of nonsense once and for all." Felix made to leave the room, but just as he reached the door Lord Romford stopped him. "Oh, and, Felix, I hope you have a reasonable explanation for your presence here in the middle of term. . . ."

"Actually, Hugo," Felix responded lightly, "I have long since learned that your opinion of a reasonable explanation differs a great deal from mine . . ." He shrugged his shoulders in helpless appeal. "And . . ."

"Enough, Felix," Lord Romford laughed. "I will speak to you later about it. I think it more expedient to talk with Miranda now."

Felix grinned mischievously. "Very well, Hugo, although I swear I'll be quaking in my boots until you have subjected me to one of your famous tongue-lashings."

Lord Romford continued to laugh after Felix had left. He was exceedingly fond of his brother and found it difficult to be angry with him for long. He remembered his own youth and the pranks he and Justin had played on various people. He was still smiling when Miranda entered and he greeted her warmly. "Miranda, my dear," he said, moving to her side, "I hope you have recovered. It must have been a terrible ordeal for you."

Miranda, surprised by the note of concern in his voice, looked at him suspiciously. She had quite expected him to be cross with her for having embroiled herself in another adventure, and found his solicitude unnerving. "I'm . . . I'm all right," she said tentatively. "At least I'm alive. That . . . that poor man, no one deserves to die like that." Her spirit returned as she spoke and she looked at her guardian defiantly. For some reason she didn't want his sympathy.

Lord Romford, as though sensing her mood, took her by the arm and led her gently to a chair. "You certainly look well enough," he said blithely. "I hope this unfortunate incident hasn't jaded your view of Wales. Normally, life is very pleasant here." Remembering her resolve to behave coolly toward him the next time they met, she withdrew her arm. She still hadn't forgiven him for being so horrid to her the last time they had seen each other. "And quite boring, I expect," she retorted. "Anyway, Anita assures me that Rodney will be happy to live in London a good deal of the time," she continued airily, "and that he won't expect me to languish here for more than a month at a time." The fact that Anita had mentioned no such thing didn't seem to weigh too heavily on her. Indeed, the lie was worth telling for she found the look of annoyance that crossed Lord Romford's face extremely satisfying.

Indeed, he was vexed by her attitude but refrained from making any comment. The last thing he wanted was to upset her.

"Is that all, Hugo?" Miranda asked. "I have to go to the library."

Lord Romford nodded. "I'll escort you," he said, offering her his arm. "I can see I don't have to tell you not to worry," he continued as lightly as possible. "I'm sure Dr. Thompson will make things as easy as possible for you and as long as you answer his questions properly the inquest will be over before you know it."

Her curiosity overcame her resolve to remain distant and she turned impulsively to him. "What is the purpose of an inquest?" she asked. "We know that a man has died and that I was the last person to see him alive. What else is there to know?"

"From what Felix has told me, I presume that in this case Dr. Thompson has to decide whether the death was accidental, or even suicide. Just remember, answer the questions to the best of your ability and don't confuse the issue by volunteering unnecessary information." He was afraid Miranda's vivid imagination would cause her to cloud the proceedings with her own theories and ideas.

"That's just as well," she said, "for I'm afraid I can't remember too much of what actually happened. When I came to, for I fainted dead away after making the discovery, you know, I saw the blood on my dress and Anita and Felix had to tell me how it got there. It's silly, isn't it, how our minds manage to suppress things that are distasteful?"

Lord Romford smiled down at her, noting for the first time the dark circles under her eyes. He realized then that she was far more upset by the incident than she acknowledged. "It is sometimes as well," he replied, "for it doesn't serve any useful purpose to dwell on the unpleasant. Shall we go?"

"Yes, I'm ready, and I'm sure poor Anita has had enough of entertaining everyone."

"Anita!" Lord Romford remarked in surprise. "Where's Mrs. Branley? Don't tell me you have driven her away!"

His tone was jocular, but Miranda thought he was serious and her temper flared. "Oh, for goodness sake, Hugo," she said angrily, "you seem to think that I'm to blame for everything that goes wrong. Well, Mrs. Branley, far from having been driven away, retired to her room with a heavy cold the moment we arrived and hasn't been seen since."

Exasperated with himself for having tried to be light, and with Miranda for misinterpreting him, he merely raised an eyebrow and walked her to the library in silence.

The conversation of all the people gathered ceased as they entered. The servants who were already seated on the straight-backed dining chairs rose, and as Lord Romford acknowledged their presence and bade them be seated again, the local squire arrived. He greeted Lord Romford affectionately.

"Glad you could get here, my boy," he said, in much the same tones he had used when Lord Romford had been a small boy. "Nasty business and am sorry that your ward made the discovery. Hope you don't think it was high-handed of me to suggest that we conduct the inquest here. Thought it would be much easier for all concerned." He turned to Dr. Thompson and drew him forward.

"May I present Dr. Thompson, Lord Romford. He has been appointed coroner."

Lord Romford acknowledged the introduction. "We met a few years back, as I recall," he said with a smile. "Up to our knees in water, fishing in the Wye."

"Heavens, yes," Dr. Thompson exclaimed. "What a miserable day that was. If my memory serves me correctly, my line broke and I lost the salmon."

Miranda moved over to Felix and Anita as the men were speaking. "Can you believe it?" she whispered furiously. "They act as though we are here for some social function. Men, they're all the same, impossible! Put them together for three minutes and they immediately start talking about sport or gambling."

Felix laughed and tweaked a stray curl on her cheek playfully. "Now, now, Miranda," he soothed, "nothing can happen until Jake arrives."

Miranda, not to be appeased, pulled away. "You're as bad as they are," she declared crossly.

"Don't tease her, Felix," Anita said quickly. "Come, Miranda, let us sit down and wait quietly. It won't do a scrap of good to work yourself up into a high dudgeon at this stage."

Jake's arrival a few minutes later brought the conversation to a close and Dr. Thompson formally opened the proceedings. Clearing his throat, he surveyed the makeshift courtroom. Satisfied that he had everyone's attention, he tucked his thumbs into his vest and began. "I want this inquest to be as informal as possible, and would appreciate it if you would remain seated until your name is called. As you know," he continued, "we are here to establish the full circumstances surrounding the death of one, Anthony Roberts. I have a few questions to ask that, I hope, will help me reach a verdict." He picked up a Bible that had been lying on a sidetable and handed it to Miranda. "Miss Haverfield," he continued, "if you would repeat after me, I swear to tell the truth, the whole truth and nothing but the truth . . ." He waited for Miranda to finish the oath and resettle herself before he continued. "Now, Miss Haverfield, I want you to tell me exactly what happened prior to your discovery of the deceased."

"I . . . I was walking home from the direction of Rossfield and I heard a gunshot," she began, the solemnity of the occasion making her feel slightly nervous. "The dogs ran off and by the time I caught up with them they had found this . . . this man under the hedge."

"Did you recognize him?"

Miranda shook her head. "No, Dr. Thompson."

"Would you be able to state with any conviction from which direction the shot came?"

Again Miranda shook her head. "No," she replied in a small voice. She was beginning to feel a little foolish at her inability to remember anything.

"Did it sound as though it were close by?"

"I'm afraid I can't recall that."

"One last question, Miss Haverfield," Dr. Thompson said kindly. "Did you see a gun lying beside the deceased?"

"No," she answered with a helpless shrug of her shoulders. "I'm sorry I cannot be of more help."

"Don't you worry your pretty head, my dear," Dr. Thompson said. "You have received a shock and I am not surprised you don't remember much of what happened. Thank you, that will be all."

Anita laid a hand on her arm. "See, I told you

there would be nothing to it," she whispered, and then sat back as Felix took the oath.

"I believe you stated that Anthony Roberts was dead when you found him," Dr. Thompson said.

"That's correct," Felix answered briskly. "By the time Jake and I reached the south field and located his whereabouts he was dead."

Dr. Thompson nodded. "Did you notice any signs of a struggle?"

"Nothing. The only flattened grass was actually under the body."

"Where was the gun when you discovered it?"

Felix paused and frowned in concentration before replying. "I think the exact placement of the weapon was to the left of the man, partially hidden by his body which would account for the fact that Miranda didn't see it."

"Quite so," Dr. Thompson said, "but please confine yourself to answering my questions and leave the conjecturing to me."

Abashed, Felix nodded.

"Do you know of any reason why Anthony Roberts would have been in the south field yesterday?"

"No," Felix responded. He had his own theory why, but wasn't going to extemporize and risk another rebuff.

"Thank you, that will be all."

Dr. Thompson then turned to the gamekeeper and once Jake had taken the oath he asked him the same question. Jake confirmed all that Felix had said.

"Did you know the deceased?" Dr. Thompson asked.

"Not well, but I knew 'im," Jake replied. "'E was well known in these parts as being something of a smuggler who 'ad fallen on bad times."

"In what way?"

"'Is family, like, moved away some months back and left 'im to fend for 'imself. From what I 'eard, 'e weren't able to cut the mustard. No one would give 'im work, so I imagine 'e turned to poaching. I 'ad reports that 'e was seen on this land a few times of late, but never did catch 'im. 'E were a bit too nimble for me."

"I see," Dr. Thompson said thoughtfully and began pacing the room. "Thank you for your help, Jake."

A silence fell on the room and after a while Miranda leaned over to Anita. "What happens now?" she asked.

"Impatient child," Anita whispered. "We have to wait for the verdict."

"Oh! Then what?"

"Then we can go and have lunch," Anita laughed in reply.

Miranda grinned back impishly at this. "I would have thought that a refined young lady would have lost her appetite after spending a morning listening to talk of dead men . . ." She broke off, suddenly aware that Dr. Thompson was waiting to speak.

"My lord, ladies and gentleman," he said grandly, once he had everyone's attention. "As I said earlier, we are here to establish the circumstances of Anthony Roberts's death. From my examination of the body and my interpretation of the answers you have so kindly given me, I believe I can deliver my verdict today. "The Honorable Felix Grey," he continued, "supplied a vital piece of evidence that confirms my own theory. He said he found the gun to the left of Roberts and I had already concluded, from the overdeveloped muscles of Roberts's left arm, that he must have been left-handed. There were burn marks on his clothing which indicated that the gun was fired at close range and," he paused dramatically, "there were no signs of a struggle. Therefore, it is my verdict that Anthony Roberts took his own life. I shall record it as death by suicide."

Lord Romford stood up and stretched his legs. He was glad it was over and that the doctor had been so quick in delivering his judgment. "Thank you, Dr. Thompson," he said. "I think I can speak on behalf of my ward and brother in saying that we appreciate your promptness in dealing with this matter, and for your agreeing to hold the inquest here."

Dr. Thompson acknowledged this with a nod of his head. "My pleasure," he said, gathering up his papers and Bible as he spoke. "Now, if you will excuse me, I must be on my way."

"Of course, although are you sure we can't persuade you to stay for luncheon?"

"Some other time," he replied. "Unfortunately, I have a few calls to make and I must be in Cardiff by five."

Lord Romford walked him to the door, extracting a promise from him to go fishing later in the week, before inviting the squire to join the party in the dining room.

The light repast had been set out in the dining room and when Lord Romford was certain that everyone had had their fill, he asked the squire if he would accompany him to the south field. "I would like to see for myself the exact spot where the poor fellow chose to die."

The squire quickly accepted and, after taking his leave, left the room with his host. Anita followed soon after, saying that she had some letters to write, and suggested that Felix take Miranda out for a ride and get some fresh air into their lungs.

"A good idea," Felix said, "for I don't fancy kicking my heels until Hugo decides he wants to see me. Go on, Miranda, get yourself changed."

"I won't be long," she said, "and let's have a race. A good gallop is just what I need." She walked upstairs quickly and as she approached her room she saw Mrs. Lloyd coming out.

"Oh! Miss Haverfield," the housekeeper said, "I found a ring in the pocket of the dress you were wearing yesterday and I just put it on your dressing table."

"Ring?" Miranda queried. "I don't remember wearing one. Thank you anyway, Mrs. Lloyd." She walked over to the dressing table and picked up the strange-looking piece of jewelry. She stared at it blankly for a few moments and then gripped the edge of a nearby chair as she recognized the bauble. "No!" she exclaimed in horror, turning it over in her hand. "No one will ever believe me that I forgot all about it." The dead man's words came back to her and she shuddered. "What ever am I to do?"

"Are you ready, Miranda?" Felix's voice reached her as he shouted from the doorway. "We haven't got all day, you know."

Miranda turned a panic-stricken face toward him. She had to tell someone what she had done and Felix was probably the only one who would understand. "Felix," she whispered, "the most awful thing has happened and I've got to talk to you."

"Well, hurry up and change and we can talk outside," Felix replied. He was anxious to leave the house before his brother returned, and was perhaps not as sympathetic toward Miranda as he might otherwise have been.

Fortunately, though, Miranda realized the impropriety of talking indoors. "I'll only be a few minutes," she said as she pulled her riding habit out of the wardrobe. "I'll meet you in the stables."

Ten minutes later, dressed in a most fashionable pale-blue velvet habit, she joined Felix.

"I say, old girl, you do look a bit peaky. What's up?"

"I'd rather wait until we reach the copse," she answered, looking meaningfully toward the grooms' quarters. "I don't want anyone to hear what I have to say."

"Heavens! What a mystery. Come, I'll give you a head start and race you there."

Miranda pulled her mount around and with a slight flick of her whip trotted out of the stables. She had almost reached the copse before Felix caught up with her, but with a final burst of speed she spurred her horse and beat Felix to their destination by a nose.

"Well done, Miranda," Felix congratulated her. "I felt for sure I would get by you." He dismounted and helped her down. "Now, tell me what has upset you."

Miranda pulled the ring out of a pocket and gave it to him. "That . . . that man gave it to me . . . the one I found and . . . and he said, 'The queen makes the straight flush,' then he fainted away, Felix, what am I going to do? I forgot all about it until just now." She spoke quickly, almost incoherently, in her anxiety to share her story.

Felix looked at her and laughed. "Do you know how ridiculous that sounds?" he gasped. "I vow no one would have believed you anyhow. I'm sure Dr. Thompson would have raised his eyes to the ceiling and thought it all ham, just the ramblings of a young lady with an overactive mind. And Hugo, well, you can just imagine what he would have said. If you want to know my honest opinion, Miranda, I think it just as well you forgot to mention it." He had stopped laughing, but it was patently obvious to Miranda that her confession had amused him immensely.

"You believe me, though, don't you?" she asked with some irritation. "It's true, every word of it. I . . . I can't think why it slipped my mind

Felix looked at the ring again and noted the curious design on the face. "Roberts said the queen made the flush, did he? I wonder what he meant, and if this design is supposed to represent a queen's head?"

"You're not laughing at me, are you?" Miranda asked, eyeing him suspiciously.

"No, of course not, my girl, I believe you, even though it does sound all a bit farfetched. But I tell you what," he continued enthusiastically, "we have ourselves a mystery to solve,"

"Shouldn't we tell Dr. Thompson?"

Felix shook his head. "There's no point until we have untangled the meaning of the cryptic message, for, of a certainty, he ain't going to like it one bit. No, I think we ought to look into this ourselves and when we have turned up something we can then present him with the additional evidence."

Miranda looked at him dubiously. "Are you sure that's the right thing to do?"

"Where's your spirit?" he teased. "We'll have a famous time acting as sleuths, and if we don't turn up anything in a week or so, we can tell Hugo and see what he advises."

The very mention of her guardian made her

stiffen. "You're right, Felix. I would feel very foolish going to Dr. Thompson now, and Hugo wouldn't believe I had forgotten. He would say I had deliberately withheld the information just so that I could get into one last scrape before my marriage."

"No matter," Felix said, not wanting to enter into a discussion about the high-handed ways of his brother. "We have more important things to do than worry about what Hugo will say. I want you to think very carefully. Are you certain that you don't remember seeing a gun by Roberts when you found him?"

Miranda shook her head. "I don't think there was one, but I can't be certain. Roberts was on his back, I think, and his body may well have concealed it, Why, is it important?"

"Very much so. You see, *if* there wasn't a gun at his side when you discovered him, but there was one by the time I arrived; it can only mean one thing. A third party put the gun there, after you had left the scene, in the hopes of covering up the fact that Roberts had been murdered."

"Murdered!" Miranda ejaculated. "You can't mean it, surely."

"Every word," he responded. "And I propose we go to the south field first thing tomorrow and see if we can find any clues."

Miranda let out a sigh. She could feel that familiar thrill of excitement she usually experienced before embarking on adventure. Only this time she felt nervous as well, for she knew the consequences would be vastly different if anything went wrong. "All right," she agreed finally, "but then we must find out more about the ring."

"That won't be as difficult as you imagine," he

replied, looking at it closely, "for I think this must have belonged to one of my ancestors. See this," he pointed to a crest that was emblazoned in one corner, "that's our coat of arms."

Five

While Miranda and Felix were making their plans for solving the mystery, Viscount Brynmawr arrived at Rossfield to find his nephew, Sir Walter David, waiting for him. The viscount, his normally handsome features somewhat marred by the lines of tiredness about his eyes, allowed a look of annoyance to cross his face as Sir Walter greeted him. He had received some disturbing news about that young man's recent activities and the last thing he wanted was to have to deal with him at this delicate time. He was anxious to begin his serious courtship of Miranda.

"Hello, Walter," he managed, carefully hiding the disdain he felt under a smile. "What brings you here?"

"I took it into my head to invite myself to stay for a few days," Sir Walter replied airily. "Heard you were expected and all that, so thought you might like the company."

"I didn't realize my arrival was of such import to cause the whole countryside to talk about it," Viscount Brynmawr remarked dryly.

"Well, actually," Sir Walter said, unabashed, "I happened to be riding this way and stopped at the Rose and Crown. Old Phelps told me you were coming down." Phelps was the landlord of the local hostelry.

"I see. How long do you plan to stay?"

Sir Walter coughed and glanced about him nervously. "A few days, Rodney, that's all." His casual use of Viscount Brynmawr's Christian name was due to the fact that only a few years separated them and they had been virtually raised as cousins.

"In a spot of trouble, are you?" The viscount asked the question, knowing the answer to be in the affirmative. The covert meeting he had had the night before last with his nephew's alleged partner left very little room for doubt in his mind that Sir Walter was engaged in some nefarious dealings. The man, Roberts, wanted money to keep quiet about it all, but the viscount was damned if he was going to part with a halfpenny to save his nephew's skin. He was supposed to meet with Roberts again on the morrow and discuss the question of payment further.

"No . . . no, not really, just a few creditors at my heel . . ." Sir Walter laughed, as though confident that the viscount would understand.

"As long as you don't look to me to bail you out, and you don't expect me to entertain you, you're welcome to stay. I'm thinking of getting married, and expect to spend a deal of time at Ramsden."

Sir Walter paled at this piece of information but

quickly offered his congratulations. "Who . . . who is the lucky lady?"

"Miranda Haverfield, Lord Romford's ward," the viscount said brusquely. He had no intention of discussing his marital plans with his nephew and sought to end the interview. "Now, if you'll excuse me, I have to change."

"D'you mind if I take the blue room?" Sir Walter asked, seemingly reluctant to be left alone.

"That's perfectly all right," the viscount answered impatiently. "Just tell the housekeeper and she'll see to everything."

"*If* I can find her," Sir Walter said sarcastically. "Honestly, Rodney, I don't know why you can't maintain decent servants here, instead of making do with the villagers. They have no understanding of how a gentleman should be looked after."

"That's enough, Walter," the viscount responded sharply. "I'll thank you to keep a civil tongue in your head while you're under my roof." He left the room quickly, determined not to waste any more time.

When he presented himself at Ramsden an hour later, the anticipation he felt at the thought of being reunited with Miranda caused him to forget all else. As he waited in the hallway for the butler to deliver his card he pulled nervously at his jacket sleeve and then mentally scolded himself for behaving like a schoolboy. He was standing thus, when the butler returned with the request that he come this way.

He was ushered into a very pleasant room. The afternoon sun was streaming through the windows, flooding the room with light. He looked round in the expectation of seeing Miranda but instead was brought up short when he saw a strange young lady approaching him. He noticed she was wearing a cap, and thought how absurdly youthful it made her look.

"Viscount Brynmawr." Her pleasant voice interrupted his thoughts. "Please forgive the informality, but I was repotting some plants."

He took another look about him and realized that he was in the atrium. "Very pleasant it is too," he said. "I'm afraid, though, you have me at a disadvantage. I don't think we have met, have we?"

"How silly of me," Anita said with a small laugh. "I'm Hugo's cousin, Anita Mayberry, and acting companion to Miranda." She gently disengaged her hand from his firm grasp. "Miranda is out at the moment. I know she'll be sorry she wasn't here to greet you."

"No matter," the viscount responded, eyeing Anita discreetly. He wondered why he hadn't met her before. "I say, I didn't commit a blunder, did I?" he asked. "I . . . I mean, we haven't met before, have we?"

Anita shook her head, her eyes alight with amusement. "No, my lord," she responded. "My father died the year I was supposed to be presented and . . . and I never did make my debut."

"That would account for it, then," he said, satisfied that he hadn't been rude. "Will Miranda be long? Or perhaps I should return later. . . ." He hesitated, in order to give Anita time to invite him to stay, which she did very readily, much to his pleasure.

"She won't be long, I'm sure. She only went out for a ride in order to clear her head. What with the inquest this morning, and Hugo's unexpected arrival, she has had quite a trying time."

The viscount's face registered signs of alarm.

"Inquest, ma'am?" he inquired. "What has happened?"

"How thoughtless of me," Anita said in distress. "For some reason I expected you to know all about it. Miranda made the dreadful discovery yesterday of a man in the south field. He . . . he had committed suicide. She is perfectly all right now," she added quickly, as she saw the troubled look on the viscount's face. "Indeed, I must confess that I was more upset than she."

"Who was he?" the viscount asked. "A local man?"

Anita nodded. "Anthony Roberts. A poacher, according to Jake."

The viscount started at the name but quickly affected a nonchalant pose and murmured, "How unfortunate. But you say Miranda has suffered no adverse effects?"

"None at all," Anita reassured him, unaware of the shock she had just delivered. "She did what she could to help him, but he died within minutes of her finding him."

"Dreadful. Quite dreadful. The coroner was quite convinced he killed himself?"

"No doubt at all. And I must say I agree with his verdict, even though no note was found. The man was down on his luck and had been unable to find work for some time."

The viscount stared at her thoughtfully, as though he were going to ask another question, but then changed his mind. "As long as Miranda is all right," he said finally, "I suppose we must be thankful. I would hate for her spirits to be depressed, for I must say it is her cheerful outlook on life I find so attractive."

Anita, suddenly conscious that she was still

holding a plant in her one hand, put it down quickly and wiped her fingers on her white apron.

"Don't let me impose on you," the viscount said hastily, as he realized with surprise that he was enjoying the picture she made, "or interrupt your work. I don't want to be held responsible if any of the plants wilt from lack of attention."

"If . . . if you don't mind, then," Anita began tentatively, "I'll just finish this geranium." She picked up an earthenware pot and deftly dropped the plant in before covering the roots with soil. "There," she said, aware that the viscount was still looking at her, "it's been given a new lease on life and I hope that next year it will show its appreciation by flowering."

"Did you ever see that still life that Watteau painted of flowers?" the viscount asked, apropos nothing. "I believe it's hanging in the Gallery at the moment. A marvelous canvas that. He used the technique of mixing oils with egg whites, only he used quail eggs to produce the luster that makes the flowers seem so realistic."

"Unfortunately, I didn't," Anita answered, "but I did see some of his other works when I was in Paris and was much taken by his style."

The viscount looked at her in surprise. It wasn't often that he met a female who was enthusiastic about art. Most women responded with a mechanical interest, but it was quite obvious to him that Anita's was genuine.

"You've visited the Louvre? Marvelous place, isn't it? I spent a week there but regrettably had to cut short my stay because of family illness."

"My visit was even briefer," Anita said, "for I went to France with my sister and had very little time to myself."

"Pity, pity. You should return."

"I have every intention of doing that," Anita said. "I have promised myself that no matter what happens I will go next year."

"Good for you, Miss Mayberry. I admire your spirit."

Anita, as though nonplused by this compliment, turned away and pretended to busy herself with tidying the workbench.

"I hear Hugo has collected a few impressive paintings," the viscount continued, unaware that he had put Anita to the blush. "Do you know where he keeps them?"

"I . . . I believe some of them are here," Anita replied softly, "although I am certain he keeps most of them in London. Ah! Here he is now, he can tell you himself."

Lord Romford walked in, and smiled when he saw the viscount. "I had no idea you were arriving so soon," he said by way of greeting. "Can I persuade you to dine with us tonight?" He turned to Anita. "Chef can manage an extra cover?" he inquired.

"Chef can manage twelve extra covers," she responded. "His grasp of English is no better than mine of Italian and unfortunately when I say, 'There will be three for dinner,' he thinks I mean thirteen. Not that we don't appreciate your thoughtfulness in providing us with a bona fide cook, Hugo," she laughed, "as long as you don't start complaining about the shockingly high household bills."

The viscount, who had been listening to this interchange with some enjoyment, broke in hurriedly. "Well, if it don't appear too rude, Hugo, I'd love to accept, only that damned, pardon Miss

Mayberry, that nevvie of mine has decided to visit. So would appreciate it if you could extend the invitation to him as well."

"But of course, Rodney," Lord Romford said. "I take it you are referring to Walter?" The viscount nodded. "I think we can manage, don't you, Anita? Shall we say five-thirty?"

"In that case I'll see Miranda at dinner. Five-thirty it is," the viscount said and tactfully took his leave.

Lord Romford left with him and Anita watched them go with a troubled expression on her face. Contrary to what she had expected from Miranda's description, she had found the viscount to be extremely interesting and exceedingly handsome. With a sigh, she turned and rang for the butler. She couldn't deny that she found him attractive, but at the same time it would simply never do to form an attachment for someone so unattainable.

Six

The dinner, being served with suitable deference
by the butler and footman, wasn't a great success
for Miranda. It certainly wasn't the fault of the food
but more to do with her inability to participate in
the conversation which naturally revolved around
the death of Anthony Roberts. Seated as she was
between Sir Walter and Viscount Brynmawr, she
could do little more than murmur monosyllabic
answers to the rash of questions Sir Walter threw
at her. Indeed, Sir Walter's interest in the whole
incident left her feeling nervous and slightly suspicious. Anita, at the opposite side of the table, was
of little help, for she appeared deep in conversation
with Lord Romford and Felix.

The viscount, in an effort to intervene and put
his betrothed at ease, frowned at his nephew as he
sought to steer the conversation into different
channels. Remembering the interest Anita had

shown in art, he asked if she too was an admirer of canvases.

"Admirer of—?" Miranda started to question until she realized what he meant. "Oh! I see what you mean. Art." She gave a small laugh to cover her stupidity. "Of . . . of course," she lied quickly, thankful to be able to turn away from Sir Walter. If the truth were to be known, she wasn't the least bit interested and knew very little on the subject. However, in order to cover her ignorance, she mentioned the names of a few artists that she knew Anita particularly admired and blushed when the viscount complimented her on her good taste.

"I see you share Miss Mayberry's enthusiasm," he said, obviously pleased to have established a common bond with her. "It will be my great pleasure to give you a personal tour of the art galleries in Europe after we are married."

"I . . . I . . . That will be wonderful," Miranda responded as lightly as she could, but the very idea of spending her honeymoon in such a boring pursuit made her shudder. "Anita will envy me forever." She knew this to be true and was able to say it with conviction.

Anita, hearing her name, looked up, her eyebrows raised in question, and Miranda, forgetting her manners, hurriedly drew her into the conversation. Anita, mindful of the viscount's interest in Lord Romford's collection, turned to her cousin with the request that they all repair to the art gallery after dinner. "For Viscount Brynmawr, I know, would like to see your new acquisitions."

Lord Romford, happy by the seeming accord his ward and the viscount had reached, agreed. The whole affair was going far more smoothly than he had thought possible and if Miranda's sudden interest in art was for the viscount's sake, then he would do his utmost to encourage it.

"There's one painting I would certainly like your opinion on, Rodney," he said. "The artist is an Englishman living in France, who has yet to gain acceptance, but I believe he will be famous one day."

"Who is he?" the viscount asked. "Has he had a showing yet?"

"No. Not here, I stumbled across his work when I was in France last year. His name is Constable and he specializes in painting landscapes."

The discussion became general and Miranda sat back, allowing her thoughts to wander. She tried to envision what her life would be like married to the viscount, but it was impossible. She had known it wouldn't work, but after tonight she knew she would fight with every weapon at her command to prevent her guardian from forcing her into the alliance.

Her musings were brought to an end when the men decided to forego the pleasure of their brandy and cigars in order to see the paintings before darkness fell.

"It's easier on the eye to see them in natural light," Lord Romford observed as he rose from the table. "If you will follow me, ladies and gentlemen," he continued in pompous tones normally associated with tour guides, "it will be my pleasure to show you the remarkable collection that is housed in the east wing. You will find it an odd assortment, family portraits side by side with masterpieces, but all reflect the eclectic taste of the Romfords."

Miranda tried not to laugh at his impersonation, and brought her handkerchief to her lips to conceal her smile. When he wasn't up in the boughs with her about her behavior, he really was quite amusing.

They all trooped out after him. Anita fell into step beside Miranda and Felix, allowing the viscount to walk with Lord Romford. No one appeared to notice that Sir Walter, who brought up the rear, looked slightly distracted. As they entered the room, the viscount and Lord Romford went immediately to inspect the Constable and after a few seconds hesitation, Anita joined them.

Miranda and Felix wandered around the room, pausing briefly every now and then to take a longer look at a few of the ancestral portraits. Sir Walter remained near the door and Miranda ignored him, determined not to encourage him to join them.

"Look at this one, Miranda," Felix said with a laugh. "Have you ever seen such a grim-looking gentleman?"

Miranda shook her head. "He's ferocious, isn't he?" She peered at the brass inscription affixed to the bottom part of the frame. "Lord Romford At Home," she read out and stood back to take another look.

"Very informative," Felix observed and was about to move on when Miranda caught his arm.

"Look at his hand, Felix," she hissed. "The ring."

They both stared in fascination, recognizing the ring instantly as the one that was now in their possession.

"What do you think it means?" she whispered, looking around to ensure no one was within earshot.

"I don't know at the moment," Felix replied softly. "But Hugo may know something."

"We can't ask him," she said quickly, not wanting to involve her guardian and risk arousing his curiosity.

"Leave it to me," Felix reassured her. "I think I can get him to talk, for he loves nothing more than delivering lectures on our family history." He patted Miranda's hand reassuringly before calling his brother over. "Hugo, come here for a moment, would you?"

Lord Romford turned in response to his brother's request. "Excuse me," he murmured to the viscount and Anita. "What is it, Felix?"

"How old is this painting?" Felix asked casually. "There's no date to indicate which Romford he is."

Lord Romford looked at the painting carefully. "That is the fourth one, and, if I'm not mistaken, this portrait was painted just after his marriage. It's over a hundred years old."

"Interesting-looking man, ain't he?" Felix observed. "What do you know about him?"

"He was a strange fellow as far as I can gather from reading his diaries," Lord Romford responded. "Forever talking in riddles and delighted in leaving cryptic notes for his family to unravel."

Miranda glanced at Felix uneasily, unaware of the interest Sir Walter was showing in the conversation.

"In fact," Lord Romford continued, "there's a legend about him which typifies his love of mysteries."

"Yes," Felix breathed, unable to mask the excitement he felt. "What is it?"

Lord Romford laughed. "It seems that in his youth he was a bit of a spendthrift. When he finally married a remarkable Welsh lady, who incidentally possessed strange powers, she persuaded him to hide a priceless collection of gold coins for the benefit of future Romford generations."

"How thoughtful of her," Miranda interposed,

momentarily diverted. "What . . . what were these strange powers she possessed?"

Felix frowned at her, evidently annoyed by the interruption. "I'm not interested in her. Just tell us if the coins were ever found."

"Don't be so beastly," Miranda retorted before Lord Romford could say anything. "I want to know." She turned to her guardian and smiled. "Please, Hugo," she begged. "Tell me."

"Actually, there's not much I can tell you about her. I gather from my forefather's later writings that she had the ability to conjure up spirits of the dead and had the uncanny knack of predicting things that nearly always came true. It was only her marriage to Romford that prevented anyone branding her as a witch."

"But what about the coins, Hugo?" Felix asked impatiently.

"Aha! That's another story. They have never been found, but then again no one has ever made a push to find them."

"What!" Miranda and Felix exclaimed in unison. "Why not?"

"Well, in keeping with his love of puzzles, Romford worked it so that to find the treasure, the ring he is wearing in the portrait had to be found first. His idea being that if whoever found it was clever enough, he could work out from the ring where the coins were hidden."

"Famous," Felix burst out, quite unable to contain himself. "Absolutely famous."

"Well," Lord Romford countered dubiously, "I'm not so certain, for the last entry in Romford's diaries refers to a curse that his delightful wife put on the finder of the ring."

"A curse?" Miranda said faintly. "Why would

she want to do something like that?" Her spirit seemed to desert her, and Felix, sensing this, gripped her arm tightly.

"Apparently she had the feeling that a Romford wouldn't find the ring. . . ."

"But what would happen if someone found it, then passed it on to another? Would that second party be cursed as well?" Felix asked quickly.

Lord Romford shook his head. "No. And presumably the treasure would be his if he were able to solve the riddle."

The relief Miranda felt at hearing these words made her quite weak and she was thankful she could use Felix as a support.

"And you never tried?" Felix asked. "I mean, to find the coins?"

"Justin and I spent all of one day, once, but I can assure you that we found it a most boring task."

"I can't think why you've never told me about this before, Hugo," Felix said. "I consider that most unfair."

"Quite honestly," Lord Romford responded, obviously amused by his brother's reaction, "it never occurred to me that you would be interested. However, now that you know, why not spend some time searching for the ring?"

"Good idea," he said heartily. "Don't you think, Miranda? We can have some fun."

Miranda, momentarily forgetting the viscount's presence, agreed. "I can't think of a more delightful way to pass the time," she said thoughtlessly, and only realized how tactless she had been when she saw the look of annoyance cross Lord Romford's face. The viscount, however, was still deep in conversation with Anita and it was quite clear that he hadn't heard.

"I don't want you losing sight of the reason for your visit here," Lord Romford said with some severity. "By all means help Felix, but not to the exclusion of all else."

Miranda could feel her temper rising, and was just about to answer when Sir Walter stepped forward.

"If I can be of any help," he said suavely, "do let me know."

Miranda started at the sound of his voice. She had quite forgotten he was there. "Thank . . . thank you," she replied, slightly flustered.

The party broke up soon after and Miranda, who genuinely felt tired, bid everyone good night. Later, as she climbed into bed and snuffed out her candle, a strange thought entered her mind. After a few moments of further reflection she decided that she could well have found the answer to her own personal dilemma of avoiding marriage to the viscount. With a little smile playing on her lips she snuggled down under the bedclothes and curled her toes in satisfaction.

Anita was the perfect wife for Rodney and she would concentrate on bringing them together when the mystery of the ring had been solved.

Seven

When Anita woke the next morning her head ached abominably. The few hours sleep she had managed had not refreshed her in the slightest. Her dreams had been of the viscount and they had been most disturbing. She threw back the covers and climbed wearily out of bed. There was only one thing she could do and that was to leave Ramsden. For her own peace of mind it was essential that she get away from the viscount's presence.

She dressed quickly, determined to seek an interview with her cousin before he went out, and hurried downstairs in search of him. A footman told her that Lord Romford was in his study and without more ado she joined him.

"Anita," he said, looking up from the papers he was working on, "you look troubled."

"The fact is, Hugo," she responded, "I must return to my sister."

"What!" Lord Romford exclaimed in tones of disbelief. "You can't possibly mean it."

"As soon as alternative arrangements can be made for a chaperone for Miranda, I'm afraid." She spoke firmly, afraid that Lord Romford would persuade her to stay.

He looked at her keenly for a moment, and she turned away from his scrutiny. "Has Miranda done anything to upset you?" he asked finally.

"Goodness gracious, no!" she answered quickly. "It's . . . it's just that my sister has written asking that I return. She's . . . she's expecting again."

"Then it's high time she persuaded Horace to untie his purse strings and hire her a permanent companion," Lord Romford remarked. "I speak for your own sake, Anita. These few weeks you have spent here have put a healthy glow into your cheeks. In fact, I don't remember ever seeing you look so well."

Anita could feel her resolve to leave faltering and it must have showed, for Lord Romford continued, "And what is more, I think it about time you stopped using your sister as a shield to hide behind every time you begin to enjoy yourself. Why don't you write and tell her that you can't get away?"

"I couldn't be so heartless," she protested, at the same time wondering if her cousin suspected the real reason behind her desire to leave. Her long conversation with the viscount last night couldn't have passed unnoticed. "Anyway, she is relying on me to help her through her confinement."

Lord Romford stepped over to her and put an arm about her shoulders. "Don't you think it's time you started to live your own life?" he asked gently. "Where do you think you'll be ten years from now?"

"I . . . I haven't given it any thought," she replied in a small voice.

"You'll still be with your sister and Horace, only instead of looking after four of her children you'll be taking care of her entire brood, which, undoubtedly, will have swelled to eleven. Is that the sort of life you want?"

Anita shook her head, the truth of his words rendering her too miserable to speak.

"Then take my advice. Stay here until you decide what it is you want to do."

"I'll have to think about it, Hugo," she replied. Yet, even as she spoke, she knew she would remain. The picture he had painted of the life that stretched ahead for her was too unbearable to contemplate.

Lord Romford smiled down at her, certain that he had managed to persuade her to reverse her plans. "We'll say no more about it, then," he said benevolently. "Now, about Miranda. Perhaps you could give me some advice. In your honest opinion, do you think she and Rodney are well suited?"

Anita stared at him, aghast. She couldn't possibly offer her advice on such a topic. "I . . . I . . . Hugo, I don't think I can answer that. You, surely, must be the one to decide."

Lord Romford laughed ruefully. "The truth is, Anita, I don't know what to do for the best. I don't want to force Miranda into an alliance that will make her unhappy, or, for that matter, Rodney."

"But he seems so deeply attached to her, Hugo . . . I just don't know what to say."

"Then it's best to say nothing. I suppose I should let things take their course and see what happens. It's just that I have the strongest feeling that when Rodney really gets to know her, he's going to suffer a terrible shock." He shrugged his shoulders. "No matter, maybe I'm being too pessimistic."

There was a brisk wind blowing when Miranda and Felix set out for the south field. They had slipped out of the house before breakfast in order to avoid being seen.

Miranda, her eyes sparkling with excitement, was munching on a piece of bread that she had taken from the kitchen. She put her hand into her pocket and withdrew another slice, which she offered to Felix. Her idea of last night contributed to her exuberance and for the first time in weeks she felt at ease with the world.

"I don't know what it is about me," she remarked, "but whenever I'm excited, my appetite increases. I declare I'm hungry enough to eat a seven-course dinner."

Felix laughed as he bit into the bread. "There's nothing to be nervous about—yet."

"Walter makes me uneasy. I swear he didn't stop asking me questions throughout dinner, and then . . . then when he offered to help out. Did you notice how bright his eyes were? And those two spots of color on his cheeks. He appeared quite agitated. If he weren't Rodney's nephew, I would suspect him of being involved in some way."

"It's odd that you should mention that," Felix said, "because I noticed he was behaving quite strangely in the gallery." He paused, and then shook his head. "We mustn't let ourselves imagine things, Miranda. If we're to get anywhere with our search, we must keep our minds clear."

They had reached the south field by now and Miranda slowed down. "Can you remember the exact spot?" she queried, experiencing a certain reluctance to proceed.

"If I'm not mistaken, it was just about here. Ah! Yes, see, here's the break in the hedge."

"What are we supposed to be looking for, anyway?" Miranda asked as she edged closer. "In all the novels I have read the plot is always obvious and everyone seems to know exactly what it is they wish to find."

While she was talking, Felix had picked up a stick and was poking about in the undergrowth. "I suppose we should look for signs of the presence of another person."

"A button that has conveniently fallen off his coat, perhaps?" she asked flippantly. "Or a piece of thread caught on a twig that is not blue?"

Felix turned to her, an exasperated expression on his face. "Miranda," he said severely, "this is real, not something culled out of a book. Now, please, be serious and see if you can locate any footprints."

"Footprints!" she exclaimed. "Now you're being silly. Of course there are footprints. Yours, mine, Jake's, Hugo's and the squire's."

Despondent, Felix sat down and idly flicked the stick across a blade of grass. "It's hopeless, isn't it? We're wasting our time here." He stared at the hedgerow, not knowing how to proceed.

"Come on," Miranda said, "let's go back to the house and take another look at that portrait. Maybe something will come to us."

Felix stood up and Miranda was brushing him down when the sounds of an approaching rider caused them both to turn. To Miranda's dismay she saw it was Sir Walter. "Bid him good-day and then let's be on our way," she whispered to Felix. "I don't want him asking me any more questions."

Even as she was speaking, Sir Walter dismounted and walked toward them.

"Good morning, Miss Haverfield, Felix. I had no idea you were such early risers. Lovely day, though, isn't it?"

"Yes," Felix responded gruffly. "We've been jolly lucky with the weather so far, what Miranda?"

"Extremely," Miranda agreed faintly.

"Taking a look at the fatal spot, I see," Sir Walter continued. "Bit sordid, isn't it?"

"No . . . yes," Felix began defensively. "Thought it a good idea to bring Miranda back so she can see how harmless it all is now, and stop the nightmares she's been having."

"Nightmares?" Sir Walter questioned, all conciliatory. "I'm sorry to hear that, Miss Haverfield. But really, you shouldn't trouble yourself about the likes of Roberts."

"You knew him?" Miranda asked innocently.

"No, no," Sir Walter replied hastily. "It was just an observation. Men of his ilk are all the same."

"I wouldn't know," Miranda said sweetly, "not having met any."

Sir Walter's eyes narrowed and he stepped closer. "Are you suggesting that I do?"

Miranda held her ground and looked up at him. "Indeed not, Sir Walter. I thought that that was what you implied." She gave a childish giggle. "I apologize for having misunderstood you."

"You must excuse her," Felix interrupted. "She's still a bit shaken from the unfortunate incident. Come, Miranda," he continued, taking her firmly by the arm. "We must return. Anita will be wondering where we are."

"Don't let me detain you," Sir Walter said with

a touch of sarcasm, and stood to one side to allow Miranda to pass.

They walked almost all the way back to Ramsden in silence. Miranda, disturbed by the encounter with Sir Walter, finally spoke.

"Felix, there is something sinister about that man. I don't know what it is, for, to be sure, he is of a perfectly respectable family and his looks are not displeasing, but I can sense a controlled violence about him that I cannot like."

"You aren't going to like this suggestion," Felix said tersely. "I want to confide the whole thing in Hugo. I have a feeling that if we continue by ourselves we're going to be in trouble before we know it."

Miranda hesitated briefly before agreeing. It was a step she didn't want to take and, indeed, would have refused to take, had it not been for the oppressive and ominous presence of Sir Walter.

They found Lord Romford in his study, still attending to his paperwork. As soon as he saw the troubled look on Miranda's face he knew something was afoot but resolved to hold his tongue no matter what the scrape she was in.

"You were both up beforetimes," he remarked casually. "I saw you leaving the house as I was dressing."

"Hugo," Felix cut in, not of a mind to exchange pleasantries, "Hugo, we want to tell you something, but you must promise not to get angry. Leastways, not with Miranda, for it was all my fault for persuading her to keep the information from Dr. Thompson until we had given ourselves a chance to collect further evidence."

"No, Hugo," Miranda chimed in quickly, "it's my fault as well. I shouldn't have listened to Felix, so

. . . so if you must be angry, then be angry with me."

Lord Romford had risen from his chair by this time and was experiencing the greatest difficulty in containing the mirth he felt. Never had he seen two such guilty-looking young people. "I daren't even hazard a guess as to what you have been up to," he laughed. "Maybe you should start from the beginning. . . ." He looked to Felix for an explanation, but it was Miranda who started.

She quickly told the story and if she noticed the slightly skeptical look that crossed her guardian's face when she confessed she had forgotten all about the ring until Mrs. Lloyd found it, she ignored it. Felix took up the tale of their discovery in the art gallery and ended with his suspicions of Sir Walter.

"It appears that I have to be grateful to Sir Walter," Lord Romford observed mildly when Felix had finished.

"Grateful!" Miranda exclaimed in astonishment. "What ever for?"

"Why, if he had behaved any differently, I doubt that it would have occurred to either of you to confide in me."

"What are we to do?" Miranda asked, ignoring this thrust. Secretly, she was relieved that her guardian was being so reasonable.

"Very little at this juncture," he replied. "I want you both to appreciate the delicacy of the situation. *If* Sir Walter is involved, the embarrassment to Rodney is going to be enormous. And that, as you can well understand, is something I would like to avoid."

"But if Sir Walter is involved, I don't see how we can avoid upsetting Rodney," Felix reasoned. "I mean, it's perfectly plain to me that a man would

only act like Sir Walter's been acting if he's got
something to hide. The way he sneaked up on us
this morning, for instance, and . . . and all those
questions he pushed on Miranda. . . ."

"Conjecture, nothing but conjecture," Lord Romford interrupted. "Even in Wales I do believe a man
is considered innocent until he is proven guilty."
He sat down again and tilted his chair back.
"However," he continued, after careful consideration of the matter, "my own personal feelings
toward Sir Walter are that he is a man not to be
trusted."

Miranda gave Felix a triumphant look. It was
somehow reassuring to know that they were not
alone in their dislike of the man. "And I thought
you would say I was allowing my imagination to run
wild," Miranda said. "I'm so pleased that we have
finally been able to agree on something, Hugo."

Both Lord Romford and Felix laughed at this
and the atmosphere, which had been quite tense up
to that point, lightened considerably.

"Who has the ring now?" Lord Romford asked
and, when Felix produced it, asked if he could see
it. "It really is a mystery," he said as he looked at
the ring. "I knew it was hidden in the house
somewhere, so the obvious conclusion one draws is
that Roberts found a way in. Would his motive
have been robbery? If so, I haven't noticed anything missing." He shook his head slightly. "I can
see that I will have to ask a few questions about this
Mr. Roberts and find out exactly who he was seen
with just prior to his death."

"Those secret passageways that Grandfather had
bricked up," Felix burst in. "Do you think they've
been opened? Come on, Miranda, let's go and find
out. I bet that's how Roberts entered."

"Before the two of you get completely carried away," Lord Romford said in quelling tones, "I think it a good idea to plan a treasure hunt. I don't want to push Sir Walter into covert action, but if we invite him to join us, we can watch him closely and maybe, just maybe, he will let slip something that will be useful."

"*If* he is involved," Miranda said with a smile.

"Touché, Miranda," Lord Romford responded with a laugh. "In the meantime, I will ask some questions in the village and endeavor not to arouse the suspicions of any guilty parties."

"I must say, Hugo, you've been very decent about this," Felix said. "I quite thought you would send us to our rooms with only bread and water for the rest of the day."

"What? And encourage Miranda to use her sheets as a rope and escape through the window. No, I'm too wise for that. Besides, it's just possible, by all working together, we can solve this whole thing without creating a scandal. Now, be off with you and start planning the hunt. I will send word to Rossfield, inviting both Rodney and Walter to join us."

Eight

Lord Romford had just finished penning the note when Viscount Brynmawr was announced.

"The very person I wanted to see," he said, standing up to greet his visitor. "In fact I was just writing to you."

The viscount acknowledged this with an uneasy smile. "Nothing serious, I hope," he said.

"No, no, it can wait. What can I do for you?"

"I was wondering if I could take another look at your art collection in daylight."

Lord Romford looked at him thoughtfully for a moment. He was surprised by the request, having expected the viscount would ask to see Miranda. "By all means, Rodney. And then, why don't you stay for lunch? Miranda will have returned by then," he added pointedly.

"Why, thank you, I would like to," the viscount

said hurriedly. "I'm sorry she's not in now, for I was looking forward to seeing her."

"She's not far away," Lord Romford remarked caustically, "she's with Felix looking for a secret passageway." They had reached the gallery by this time and Lord Romford stepped back to allow the viscount to enter. "Take your time, Rodney," he said. "I would like your opinion on some of the paintings."

The viscount nodded briefly and walked to the Constable. "You are right about this artist; he *will* be famous one day," he remarked. "The detail he has achieved is marvelous." There was no doubting the sincerity of his admiration. He moved on and inspected a few more paintings before pausing in front of the portrait of the fourth earl.

Lord Romford, intrigued by this display of interest, looked at it himself more closely. For the first time he noticed that his ancestor was holding some playing cards and the dead man's words came back to him. He wondered if there was a connection. It certainly would be consistent with the old man's love of mysteries. Vowing to return later when the viscount had gone, he looked over the rest of his collection. Suddenly, something seemed odd and after closely inspecting a few more canvases he realized that three of them were reproductions. He looked to see if the viscount had also noticed, but as the viscount made no mention of this phenomenon, he decided to say nothing for the time being. The viscount's silence was puzzling though, for as an acknowledged art expert it should have been something he would have noticed immediately.

"You approve, Rodney?" he asked softly.

"Very much so, Hugo," the viscount said with

apparent enthusiasm. "I envy you. If I had the financial resources, I would certainly make you an offer for a couple of them." He shrugged his shoulders ruefully and was about to make a further comment when the door opened and Miranda entered. The two men failed to recognize her for a moment, dressed as she was in a pair of breeches and a beige crepe shirt. Her hair, tied carelessly at the nape of her neck in a black ribbon, made her look like a young boy.

"Hugo, you'll never believe this. . . ." she began, but as soon as she saw the viscount she broke off. "Hello, Rodney. I didn't know you were here."

The viscount, as much startled by her dress as by her careless greeting, moved to her side. "Miranda," he said thickly, "how utterly charming you look. I . . . I was afraid that that tiresome nephew of mine had quite worn you down last night with all his questions."

"How thoughtful of you, Rodney," she murmured, forcing herself to smile as she struggled to compose herself. She was aware of the disapproving look her guardian was casting in her direction and now regretted that she had given in to the impulse to dress in Felix's clothes. "Thank you. I'm . . . I'm perfectly well."

"Perhaps you would like to take a turn in the garden," the viscount suggested, and then turned to Lord Romford for approval.

"I . . . that is, I particularly wanted to speak to Hugo . . ." Miranda said, casting a despairing look at Lord Romford.

"I'm sure it can wait," Lord Romford said coldly. "I'll be in the library when you want me, Miranda. Now, if you'll excuse me." He had just reached the door, when it opened and Sir Walter walked in.

Lord Romford surveyed him haughtily for a few moments, while the viscount frowned at this unexpected intrusion.

"Good morning, my lord," Sir Walter said. "I am looking for Rodney, and your footman told me he was with you." He brushed a lace-edged handkerchief across his brow and Lord Romford cast a look in the viscount's direction. Sir Walter continued, "You are needed back at Rossfield."

The viscount arched his brows but refrained from asking why. Instead, he turned to Miranda and took her hand in his. "Forgive me," he murmured. "I'm afraid I'll have to cry off from luncheon, but mayhap we can take our stroll later."

"Yes, yes, of course," Miranda replied, secretly relieved that their têta-à-tête had been postponed.

"Shall we go, Walter?" the viscount asked mildly. "You can tell me what is amiss on the way over."

"Before you go," Lord Romford interjected, "Miranda is organizing a treasure hunt for those coins, and we were wondering if you would both care to join in the fun."

Sir Walter cast Miranda a cool look, but she avoided his gaze.

"I don't know, Hugo," the viscount responded slowly. "Your talk of the curse is quite off-putting. What would happen if Miranda were the one to find the ring? I don't like it one bit."

Miranda blushed and looked to Lord Romford to reply.

"It's not something we should take that seriously," Lord Romford said. "After all, no one really believes in that nonsense, do they?"

"I certainly don't," Miranda said. "And the chances of finding anything are slim. It's . . . it's just that my imagination has been fired up by the talk of hidden gold and . . . and I thought to have one last, tiny adventure before . . . before . . . "

". . . Exactly, before you take on all the responsibilities of a respectably married young lady," Lord Romford concluded for her.

"Please, Rodney," she begged prettily, "please say yes."

The viscount smiled at her indulgently. "How can I refuse? Of course I'll be delighted, if it makes you happy."

"Walter?" Lord Romford asked.

Sir Walter, with a show of reluctance, shrugged his shoulders. "It strikes me as a great waste of time, but . . . if it pleases Miss Haverfield. . . ."

"Wonderful," Miranda exclaimed, clapping her hands in a show of pleasure. "What about tomorrow?"

Lord Romford shook his head. "I will not be back from London. . . ."

"London?" Miranda asked, unable to contain her surprise at this unexpected piece of news. "I didn't know you were leaving us so soon, Hugo," she recovered quickly. "I thought you said you were off next week."

"I received some news this morning that has necessitated a change in my plans," he said smoothly. "I shall only be gone a week, so shall we make plans for the hunt for when I return . . . say, in eight days?"

Both the viscount and Sir Walter nodded, and before either of them could remark on Lord Romford's trip, he deftly bid them good-day and showed them out.

Miranda was in less than a tranquil state of mind by the time Lord Romford rejoined her, with Felix in tow. It was typical of her guardian's thoughtlessness to spring such a surprise on her in front of Sir Walter.

"What has occurred, Hugo," she demanded, "that takes you away so suddenly?"

Lord Romford ignored this outburst as he raised his quizzing glasses to his eyes and surveyed her dress. "That, my dear Miranda," he drawled, "is not as important a question as the one I have for you. What explanation do you have for dressing so outrageously?"

"I can hardly crawl through dusty tunnels in my muslins," she said defensively. "And how was I to know Rodney would call this morning? I promise I will be more careful in the future."

"I will say no more on the matter, then," Lord Romford replied. "As for my trip to London, I think I know what Roberts was up to. . . ."

"Really," Miranda retorted, still smarting from her guardian's criticism.

"These three paintings," Lord Romford continued, ignoring her interruption. "They are reproductions. Someone has cleverly exchanged them and, I suspect, sold the originals."

"It had to be Roberts," Felix declared. "And he must have entered by the secret passage, for Miranda and I have just discovered that they have been unblocked."

"Why do you have to go to London?" Miranda asked, not at all pleased that she was to be excluded from this part of the adventure. "If Roberts had stolen them, surely he would have sold them in . . . in Newport or Cardiff."

"My dear Miranda, nobody in either of the two towns you just mentioned would be able to afford to buy such masterpieces. They had to be disposed of in London."

"But not by Roberts, surely," Miranda persisted.

"Exactly my thoughts," Lord Romford agreed, "but a few questions posed to the right people in London should give me all the information I need to identify the person, or persons, who sold them . . . if indeed they have been sold."

"Oh!" Miranda said, somewhat abashed. "Do you think Sir Walter is the one?"

Lord Romford nodded. "But without proof we can do nothing."

"And . . . and do you suppose that Roberts found the ring and happened onto the hiding place of the coins?"

"I think we have to assume that," Lord Romford said.

"Then," Miranda concluded triumphantly, *"if* he was working for Sir Walter, there is the possibility that Sir Walter knows of the hiding place as well."

"Good heavens!" Felix declared in admiring tones, "that is a clever piece of deduction. Why didn't I think of that?"

"You don't read enough novels," Miranda said with a laugh.

"There is only one flaw to that argument," Lord Romford said after a slight pause. "I doubt that Walter would still be gracing us with his presence if he had the coins. No, it is more likely that Roberts kept his find a secret. As a local man he would have known of the legend, so perhaps he decided to keep the treasure for himself."

"Even that doesn't make sense," Miranda argued. "I mean if Roberts was the only one to know of the hiding place, what motive would anyone else have had to kill him?"

"I have it," Felix said smugly. "How about if Roberts threatened to expose Sir Walter, unless Sir Walter gave him a bigger cut of the proceeds."

"Why would he risk that, when the coins would have made him extremely wealthy?" Miranda said in disagreement.

Lord Romford, obviously impressed by his ward's display of logic, sought to answer her. "Greed," he said. "Roberts, a man not used to wealth, would always want more. However, until we have more facts, we cannot possibly arrive at any satisfactory conclusion. First, I have to establish that Walter is the man we want, and then, when I return from London, I can proceed with my investigation and try to establish a connection between Roberts and Walter. Someone in the village, I am certain, will know something."

Miranda, again annoyed by her guardian's intrusion into what she considered her affair, gave vent to her indignation. But Lord Romford, aware of the dangers ahead, silenced her with a frown. "Bear in mind, Miranda," he said sternly, "that you came to me for help and advice. I don't want you doing anything untoward that will arouse Walter's suspicions while I am away."

"Oh, very well, Hugo," she said in aggrieved tones, "but you have no objections if Felix and I try to find the coins?"

"As long as you contain your activities to the house, no. However, by the same token, I don't want you ignoring Rodney. You are to be here to receive him when he calls."

Miranda nodded. Of course she would see him, but she would ensure that Anita was with her. At least, with Hugo out of the way, she could put that part of her plan into action.

"There is one thing you can put your deductive powers to," Lord Romford continued. "I noticed this morning that the fourth earl is holding some playing cards in his hand. Maybe you can work out a connection between them and Roberts's last words. . . ."

Felix, intrigued by this suggestion, walked over to the portrait and studied it. "You may be onto something, Hugo," he said, all admiring. "We'll do our best, won't we, Miranda?"

"As card games have been omitted from my education, you'll have to teach me first," she replied. "What type of game would call for a queen to make a flush?"

Lord Romford withdrew as Felix, with a show of impatience, began explaining the finer points of poker to Miranda. Glancing at his fob watch, Lord Romford saw that it lacked but five minutes to noon and quickly decided that if he left within the hour, he could cover a good distance of the journey to London before nightfall.

Nine

By Miranda's reckoning, her guardian would arrive back on the morrow, and as neither she nor Felix were any nearer to solving the mystery surrounding the ring, she found herself looking forward to his return. Felix had managed to enjoy himself by making great sport of exploring the secret passageway. He had discovered a secondary, far smaller one, connected to the main artery by a narrow flight of stone steps, which ended in the bedroom Miranda was occupying. They had had a fierce argument after this, for Felix was all for changing rooms just in case someone else knew of its existence. Miranda had been adamant in denying this request, though. The reason she gave Felix for her stubbornness was that Anita would, of a certainty, ask questions which could only serve to complicate matters. In reality, though, she wanted to be the one to discover if anyone did use the tunnel.

"It could be dangerous, Miranda," Felix argued furiously. "Hugo would never forgive me if anything happened to you."

"I promise to call for help if I hear any peculiar noises, but I simply refuse to move. Anyway, I think you are being an alarmist and I won't listen to another word of your nonsense."

Felix looked most unhappy and only relented when Miranda agreed to keep a bell at her bedside. "And mind you ring it, my girl, if you hear anything at all."

Nothing had happened and the tedium of having to wait for Lord Romford's return was making her restless. Had it not been for the astonishing success of her other plan, she would have been tempted to take matters into her own hands.

As it was, the viscount had called every day, and every day she had persuaded Anita to sit with them. "For propriety's sake," she had said. Even then, Anita had shown a strange reluctance to comply, and it was only after Felix declared that he certainly wasn't going to play nursemaid that she finally capitulated.

It was highly satisfying for Miranda to witness the subtle change in the viscount's attitude toward her. He no longer sat and stared at her as though she were some rare object to be admired. In conversing with him, she deliberately pretended an ignorance on most of the topics he raised, which forced him to turn to Anita and solicit her opinions. And today, she had purposely sought sanctuary in the library in order to give the viscount some time alone with Anita.

She smiled contentedly to herself and for the first time wondered what her guardian's reaction would be when he realized what had happened. "One of fury, no doubt," she mused, "that once again I have managed to thwart his plans." She sighed, suddenly aware that her immediate future was going to be bleak. She was prepared for the inevitable letdown her spirits would experience after all the excitement died down, but could she bear to be at odds with Lord Romford again? "It's always the same," she muttered, "and I cannot understand why it should be so." A thoughtful expression settled on her face as she pondered this and idly picked up the book that was lying in her lap and fanned the pages.

"That's no way to treat such a work of art, Miranda," Anita's voice interrupted her. "Here, let me have it and I'll put it away before Hugo notices that you have marked the binding."

Miranda looked up guiltily. "Oh, dear! I didn't realize what I was doing. Thank goodness you arrived before I damaged it more."

Anita took the book and carefully ironed the crease with her fingers. "Miranda, I want to talk with you."

"You sound so serious, Anita. Have I done something to upset you?"

"Yes . . . no," Anita began haltingly. "I must beg you to pay more attention to Rodney when he visits. You cannot expect me to entertain him and . . . and what's more, I do believe you are purposefully representing yourself falsely."

With a show of innocence, Miranda opened her eyes wide. "You are talking in riddles, Anita," she said.

"No, I'm not, and well you know it," Anita responded feelingly. "I'm aware that your knowledge of art is scant, but . . . but . . . to sit there and profess that you are ignorant of Shakespeare when I know how much you admire his works is too much for me to bear. It is as though you are deliberately setting out to destroy Rodney's admiration of you."

Miranda shrugged her shoulders. "Anita, he has to realize at some point that we will not suit. Surely it is kinder if I let him down gently, than be so abrupt that he will forever be unhappy. Already, I can sense that his infatuation for me is wearing thin. In another week he'll be wondering why he ever thought he wanted to marry me."

"That a man should be so ill-used," Anita snapped in an unusual display of temper. "And Hugo, have you given any thought about what he will have to say? Really, Miranda, I beg you, do not be so impetuous. Give Rodney a chance to prove that his love for you is true."

"To what avail?" Miranda said and then stopped as she saw Anita struggling to compose herself. "Very well, Anita," she continued, "I promise to try harder. But, I swear if he suggests we play chess or another hand of piquet, I'll . . . I'll . . . I'll just have to refuse, for you are well aware of my dislike of both games."

Anita gave her a watery smile. "Thank you, Miranda. I know you won't regret it." She walked over to the ladder that was before one of the book stacks. "Which shelf does this belong on?" she inquired in a voice that sounded as though she was determined to be cheerful at all costs.

"The third one down, five in from the right," Miranda responded as she watched the graceful way in which Anita ascended the steps. *A perfect match,* she thought. *I'll be able to bear with Hugo's anger because I know Anita and Rodney will be so happy together.*

Anita was still atop the ladder when Felix burst into the room. "I say, Miranda," he said excitedly, "I've just made the most famous discovery."

Miranda quickly put her finger to her lips and jerked her head in Anita's direction. "Don't tell me, let me guess," she interposed. "You . . . you have found the coins."

"No, don't be silly," Felix said, turning his back on Anita in order to mouth his thanks to Miranda.

"Well . . . no, it can't be that," Miranda continued, playing for time. "I give up. What is it?"

"Sarah has had her puppies," he said, a triumphant gleam in his eyes. "Nine of them and they're perfect. Come and see them immediately."

Miranda stood up. "You'll excuse me, Anita?" she asked sweetly and left the library before Anita could respond.

"I hope Sarah really has whelped," she whispered to Felix as they crossed the hall. "Else Anita will think you very odd."

A footman sprang to attention and opened the front doors for them.

"I'm not such a greenhorn. Of course she has. Jake told me before breakfast and I forgot to mention it to you. Anyway, that's not important. I've just come from Tintern, where I discovered that Sir Walter is in dire financial trouble."

"You beast," Miranda burst out. "How dare you leave me behind?"

"Don't get on your high horse, old girl. Anita asked me to go and do a few errands for her and I stopped in at the Rose and Crown for a pick-me-up. Before I knew it, Phelps was bending my ear about the strange carryings-on of Sir Walter and how it was common knowledge that his pockets are to let. He dropped a bundle at the gaming tables in

Cardiff, according to Phelps and . . . and what's more, Phelps swears he saw Sir Walter and Roberts together on more than one occasion." He stopped for breath. He had such a pleased grin on his face that Miranda couldn't help but laugh.

"Well, that certainly confirms our suspicions about Sir Walter," she said in grudging forgiveness. "Did he have anything else to say?"

Felix scratched his head thoughtfully. "No, he was called away to tend to a guest, but one of the locals in the bar said something which simply doesn't make sense."

"Go on," Miranda prompted.

"Actually, he wasn't talking to me, but I happened to overhear."

"Aha! Eavesdropping. No wonder you are a little reluctant to repeat such gossip."

"Do you or do you not want to hear?" Felix asked in exasperation.

Miranda nodded.

"The old man said to his friend something about the weird comings and goings at Rossfield. That's when my ears pricked up. I kept my back to him and pretended an interest in a pamphlet on the bar, not wanting to appear as though I was listening. . . ."

"Felix," Miranda said severely, "if you don't come to the point soon, I'm going to box your ears. . . ."

"His friend grunted a reply, but then this first man continued and said how Sir Walter wasn't the only one to be seen with Roberts. He claimed that he himself saw Rodney in Tintern, with Roberts, the day before Roberts died. . . ."

"Are you sure?" Miranda questioned in disbelief.

"Definitely," Felix said in positive tones.

"But . . . but . . . Rodney didn't arrive until the

day of the inquest," Miranda protested.

"Maybe that's what he wants us to think," Felix interrupted. "Just suppose that he and Sir Walter are working together . . . it's possible that Rodney would want to keep dark about his movements."

"Rodney and Sir Walter!" Miranda repeated in amazement. "Oh! Felix, you don't know what you are saying." She gave a little laugh. "Why, I've known Rodney for years and he just isn't capable of intrigue."

"Before you defend your betrothed so hotly . . ."

"He's not my betrothed," Miranda snapped, suddenly out of patience with Felix.

". . . Let me finish telling you what else I heard," Felix continued. "After saying that about Rodney, the old man proceeded to give a detailed account of a clandestine meeting he witnessed between Rodney and Roberts."

"It could hardly have been clandestine if there were onlookers. Anyway, I think it all a hum, and am disinclined to believe any of it."

Felix looked a little sheepish at this. "Actually, he didn't say it was clandestine, but that's the impression I received. Why else would Rodney have met with Roberts outside the village by the old pond?"

"Your trouble, Felix, is that you color your stories until there's not an ounce of truth left in them. If Rodney were in Tintern a day or so earlier than we expected him, I'm sure he will have a perfectly reasonable explanation. And, if the meeting you talk about did take place, it could well have been accidental. How long did it last? Did the man make mention of that fact?"

"All right, all right, Miranda. I'm sorry I mentioned it. Only I thought it most peculiar, especially if Rodney were here for two days before calling at Ramsden. For a man supposed to be in love with you he showed a remarkable lack of interest in seeing you."

"I'm sorry, Felix," Miranda apologized, aware that she had overreacted. The very suggestion that Rodney was involved was too awful to contemplate. If it were true, then all she had done to bring Anita and him together was for naught. And the anguish Anita would suffer would be entirely her fault. "I hope you understand my astonishment at your news. Rodney was such a good friend of Justin's and he's known Hugo for an age. It's difficult to imagine that he would embroil himself in such a caper as stealing his neighbor's art collection.

"And possible murder," Felix added in a serious voice. "But put in that light, I have to agree with you." He kicked a stone savagely. "Devil take it, though, I would dearly love to know what it's all about."

"So would I. However, I think we should wait for Hugo to return before saying anything. Meantime, if the opportunity arises, I can ask Rodney when he left London and when he arrived here. If he seems to be the slightest bit evasive, we'll know something is up. Now," she said, "where are the puppies?" Her head ached and she wanted nothing more than to retire to her room, but she could hardly return to the house without seeing them.

"They're in Firefly's stall. Don't try picking them up, Sarah might attack you."

She gave him a withering look as she swept past him. "Really, Felix, you forget that I'm country bred."

Sarah growled as she heard them approach and Miranda uttered a few words of comfort. "There,

there, old lady. We're not going to disturb you."
She stopped a few feet short of the dog and knelt
down on the straw that had been scattered about
the cobblestoned floor. She could see some of the
puppies, happily pulling at their mother's teats and
heard them grunting in satisfaction. For some
inexplicable reason she felt tears in her eyes and
had to blink rapidly, several times, to stem the flow.
It was such an intimate scene to witness and it
made her feel very lonely. "You clever girl," she
whispered huskily. "They're beautiful." She stood
up and, keeping her back to Felix, retreated. She
certainly didn't want him to see her crying. She
took a deep breath and felt her composure return.
"Do you think Hugo will let me have one?" she
asked. "Just think what a picture I'd make with a
liver and white spaniel prancing at my heels."

"For a country girl you show a remarkable lack
of feeling for the poor animal," Felix said, still
peeved by her earlier quip. "A spaniel needs open
spaces, not confinement."

"Don't be out of sorts with me, Felix," she
begged. "I don't mean to be such a crosspatch."

Felix laughed, his good humor restored. "You
certainly aren't the Miranda of old," he teased. "If
it's your engagement that's causing you to behave
so, I'll have a word with Hugo and tell him it won't
work."

It was Miranda's turn to laugh. "Do you think he
would listen?"

"I'll make him," Felix replied.

"No, no, Felix," she said wearily. "I can work this
out by myself, but thank you anyway." The last
thing she wanted was Felix to intervene on her
behalf, for that really would anger Hugo. Anyway,
she wasn't anxious to continue with her plans for

Anita, at least until she was satisfied that Rodney wasn't involved. She would simply have to accept the viscount's courtship for a while longer.

"I'm going to rest," she said. "My head aches and I'm in no mood to see Rodney if he calls."

"I hope you haven't caught Mrs. Branley's cold," Felix said in an attempt to cheer her up. "We can't have you retiring to your bedchamber for a week."

Miranda gave a faint smile. "I had almost forgotten she was here. I suppose I should really go and visit her."

"What! And give her palpitations. She refused Anita's offer yesterday to sit with her for a while. So I don't think she'll welcome your company. Personally, I think she enjoys being miserable."

"Poor Mrs. Branley. I have been an awful burden for her and I shall try to be less trying in the future."

Felix looked at her in surprise. "My, my," he said. "This is a turnabout. Hugo will be pleased to learn that you intend to mend your ways."

Miranda punched him playfully on his arm. "All I said was that I would try. I don't, however, think I will succeed. If you see Rodney, apologize for my absence." She walked quickly back to the house and slipped inside through a side entrance in an effort to avoid meeting Anita.

Ten

The rain, which had been a light drizzle most of the morning, turned into a downpour. Lord Romford cursed loudly as he pulled his tricorn further down on his head and turned up the collar of his caped cloak. Even so, small rivulets of water found their way down his neck and after twenty minutes he abandoned his plans of making Ramsden that day.

Luckily, the next village he came to sported a reasonable inn and after ensuring that his horse was well taken care of, he entered the warmth of the taproom and ordered a brandy.

"Nasty day, it be," the landlord, a large, ruddy-faced individual, remarked pleasantly as he helped Lord Romford out of his wet overclothes. "I'll 'ave a room for you in a trice, sir," he continued, and recognizing the nobility of his guest by the superfine quality of his clothes added, "You'll be wanting a private sitting room, I suppose?"

"No, no, I don't expect to stay more than one night," Lord Romford replied. "This will suffice. Indeed, it is a very cozy room." The inclement weather had caused the landlord to light a fire, which made it very pleasant.

The landlord, warmed by the compliment, bowed. "We like to make our patrons feel at 'ome," he responded cheerfully, as he poured the brandy into a large glass. "I'll send the wife in and you can tell 'er what it is you'll be wanting to eat. The food's plain, m'lord, but wholesome." He hurried out, calling to his wife as he went.

Lord Romford sipped at his drink thoughtfully and walked to the fireplace. His trip to London had been a waste of time and he was angry with himself for assuming that it would be easy to get the information he wanted. All he had been able to ascertain was that a dealer with a highly dubious reputation had bought the paintings, but who he bought them off still remained a mystery. His several attempts to meet with the man had been fruitless and he had finally been forced to leave his own agent in charge of tracking the dealer down.

One thing he had resolved, though, was that he would not force Miranda into marriage. He had given the matter considerable thought and had come to the conclusion that the viscount would not make a suitable husband for his wilful ward. Actually, it had taken Henrietta to point this fact out to him two nights ago when they had met at the Denbighs' soiree. Once she had spoken her mind, he had been forced to agree with her.

The viscount's name had come up when somebody had asked his whereabouts because they wanted a painting evaluated. Lord Romford mentioned that he had repaired to his estates in Wales. He hoped to end the conversation there. But it was not to be, for someone else, who had been present at the fateful Vauxhall rout, related the story of that evening and the forthcoming marriage. Henrietta, who had been standing to one side, glanced at Lord Romford and gently shook her head. Later, when the crowd had thinned, he managed to draw her to one side and ask her what she had meant.

"My dear Hugo, I'm surprised that you would countenance such a match. Rodney's a very sweet man, but your ward will eat him alive. She is far too vivacious for him."

"I don't think it will come to that, Henrietta," he laughed. "Miranda is not a cannibal."

"Don't joke about such things," Henrietta replied with mock severity. "I know how awful such marriages can be, for don't forget I suffered one just the same. Percy was a lamb but never did understand me and I made him miserable most of the time."

"And you, my dear," he said gently, "if I recall correctly, were just as unhappy."

"Then you begin to perceive the validity of my claim, Hugo?" she asked.

He bowed gracefully and briefly touched her hand. "The final decision must be Miranda's, but I shall inform her that if she wishes to call off the engagement, I will support her." He wondered, even as he spoke, why he had agreed so readily to do as Henrietta suggested, for in general he was not so biddable. Was it because Miranda reminded him of Henrietta? Her innocence notwithstanding, there was a similarity and he didn't want to take the risk that she, through no fault of her own, would end up like Henrietta.

Neither he nor Henrietta mentioned the letter that had ended their brief affair. There had been no need, for both understood the rules that governed such relationships. It was enough that they could remain friends and enjoy each other's company in public.

The arrival of the landlord's wife broke into his reverie and he took another sip of his drink as he listened to a recitation of the food she had to offer.

"The saddle of mutton will suffice," he responded, "and perhaps some cheese."

"Thank 'ee kindly, m'lord. I'll 'ave it ready for 'ee in a while."

"I'm in no hurry. If you'll be kind enough to show me to my room, I think I'll change before dining."

"Of course, m'lord," she said, curtsying as she spoke. "If you'll just follow me, I think you'll find everything to your satisfaction. It's not often we get landed gentry staying 'ere, but, even if I say so meself, I keep a nice, clean 'ouse."

The shining horse brasses and well-scrubbed flagstone floors bore out the truth of this statement and Lord Romford smiled at the woman as he walked past her to the door. "I'm sure I'll be more than comfortable."

The next morning as he set out for Ramsden, he felt as refreshed as if he had spent the night in his own bed. Making a mental note of the name of the inn, the Crow's Foot, he decided that if the opportunity ever arose, it would be an ideal place to spend a discreet weekend. The countryside was beautiful and after the heavy downpour of yesterday, the greenery was lush.

His horse, as well rested as he, was ready for exercise and two hours later they were approaching Tintern. Instead of heading for Ramsden, Lord

Romford guided his horse in the direction of Rossfield. A sudden whim to consult the viscount about Miranda was responsible for his decision and it only occurred to him that he could question his host further about his knowledge of art as he was being ushered in five minutes later.

The viscount greeted him warmly and called for some refreshments. "Might be awhile, though, Hugo, for my servants are not as well trained as yours."

"No matter, Rodney. A mug of ale to quench my thirst would be welcome, but I'll conserve my appetite for lunch at Ramsden." He waited as the viscount issued instructions to a servant, before he came to the point of his visit. "Have you seen much of Miranda?" He watched the viscount's face carefully as he spoke and saw the look of tension that sprang into his eyes.

"Every day," the viscount responded briefly. "She is well, full of the treasure hunt and . . . and . . . life. She is an amazing young lady."

Not quite the description one would expect to hear from a man in love, Lord Romford thought wryly. *Maybe his infatuation is wearing off.* "I won't waste your time, Rodney," he said briskly. "The purpose of my call is to inquire whether you are really set on marrying the chit."

The viscount stared at him blankly for a moment. Relief, mingled with despair, seemed to envelop him. "I . . . I . . . think, that is, of course I am, Hugo. I'm aware that it was my deliberate and foolish gesture that has put Miranda into such an awkward position. I would not dream of playing her false now."

This answer satisfied the last nagging doubt that Lord Romford entertained about the viscount's feelings toward Miranda, but realizing that he would be foolish to push the matter further, he decided to tell Miranda that she could call off the engagement and put Rodney out of his misery. The viscount was no more in love with her than he was and would undoubtedly welcome the end to such a farce. "I'm sorry I mentioned it, Rodney," was all he said. "By the way, Cecil Rutledge was looking for you. I saw him at the Denbighs'."

"Wanted me to evaluate a painting for him, no doubt," the viscount observed. "He's a cheese-paring sort of fellow. Rather ask my advice than pay an agent."

"I'm told you are a nonpareil when it comes to spotting a fake," Lord Romford said nonchalantly, "so I'm glad that my collection at Rossfield passed your scrutiny."

The viscount seemed to pale at this and quickly turned away. "I . . . I didn't look at your collection closely enough to . . . to detect anything wrong," he stuttered. "Anyway, Cecil has exaggerated my abilities. I'm afraid I wouldn't be able to tell the real thing from a good reproduction. Only an expert has that capability."

"You are too modest, Rodney," Lord Romford said suavely. "Cecil is not the only one to hold you in such high esteem. Prinny himself talks of you in the most glowing terms. Claims he doesn't buy a painting without first asking your advice."

The viscount had the grace to demur, but it was obvious the conversation was making him edgy. He coughed nervously and looked pointedly at the clock on the mantelshelf. It was almost noon.

"I see I must be on my way," Lord Romford said. "Otherwise I'll be late for luncheon. Do we see you tonight for dinner?"

Looking more uncomfortable than ever, the viscount shook his head. "No, Hugo, but thank you for the invitation. I have to go to Newport on business this afternoon and do not expect to return until late."

"Tomorrow, then," Lord Romford pressed, "for the treasure hunt?"

"Yes, yes, of course. Tomorrow."

Lord Romford rode away slowly. The viscount's evasiveness was puzzling, unless he knew something about the missing pictures. Shrugging his shoulders, he urged his horse to a gallop and arrived at Ramsden in time to join the others for lunch.

The atmosphere in the dining room was heavy and when he walked in he was surprised by the warmth with which Miranda greeted him. Both she and Anita looked pale, and Felix, with forced cheerfulness, begged him to be seated, "dust and all."

"If you ladies can bear with me in such a state," he said pleasantly, "I think I will, for until now I hadn't realized how hungry I was."

Miranda wrinkled up her nose. "I think we can, this once, do you not agree, Anita?"

Anita smiled wanly as the footman quickly set another place. "Pray be seated, Hugo," she said in an attempt to match Miranda's humor, "otherwise I shall feel compelled to eat my fingernails to ease the gnawing pangs of hunger."

Lord Romford laughed and sat down. "Has anything happened in my absence? There seems to be a general air of despondency about you all."

Miranda looked at Felix quickly and frowned. "That's just it, Hugo, nothing has happened of any consequence. We are no nearer to solving the mystery of the coins than when you left. I can quite see why you and Justin became disenchanted with your search so quickly."

"I think it's all fudge," Felix said grumpily. "Something the fourth earl made up. A figment of his overripe imagination."

"My, my," Lord Romford observed, "we are in a state of depression. Do you want to cancel the hunt? Although I have just come from Ramsden and Rodney assured me he is looking forward to it."

"No, we can't do that," Miranda said hastily. "Even though the search will be fruitless. I have come up with some false clues that will keep you all busy guessing. Anita has even had the foresight to make up a set of coins which I have hidden at the end of my trail."

"And Mrs. Branley? How is she?" Lord Romford asked this, thinking that perhaps the elderly lady had been troublesome.

"On the mend," Anita replied. "Mrs. Lloyd informed me this morning that she is almost ready to brave the fresh air."

"The rain yesterday caused her to retreat, though," Miranda added mischievously.

"I can quite understand that," Lord Romford said. "Even I decided to retreat and spent the night in a most delightful inn."

"You had more reason, Hugo," Miranda said. "You, at least, were outside. Mrs. Branley has been cooped up in her room for three weeks with not even a window open."

"Now, now, Miranda," Anita chided, "I'm sure she'll join us when she feels better."

"And that will be too soon for Miranda," Felix teased. "But, enough of that. How was your trip, Hugo?"

"A fruitless errand, I'm afraid, but, no consequence, I shall find other paintings to buy," he added for Anita's benefit. "Has word arrived from Captain Jones yet?"

"Just this morning," Felix responded, pausing to take a draft of ale. "He sent a young lad by the name of Tim over. They made port two nights ago. In fact, there's a letter for you in your study."

Lord Romford nodded. "We can ride over at the weekend and take a look at *The Owl* if you like, Felix."

"Would I ever?" Felix declared enthusiastically. "Maybe I could take her out into the Channel."

"As long as Anita and I are invited, we could sail to Ireland," Miranda interrupted, obviously displeased at being excluded.

"Not me," Anita said quickly. "I'm a hopeless sailor and only take to the high seas under the greatest provocation."

Miranda and Felix continued to squabble about where they would sail and Lord Romford sat back, smiling indulgently. He was pleased to see that Miranda had regained her spirits, but Anita's withdrawn expression indicated that something had happened to upset her. He stood up, excusing himself on the pretext of wanting to read Captain Jones's note, and left the room.

He wanted to see Felix alone. Maybe he could shed some light as to why Anita appeared so miserable.

The letter was propped up on his desk and breaking the seal he quickly glanced through the two pages of almost illegible writing before settling down to read it. The brief report about *The Tawny Owl*'s performance was succinct, but then toward the bottom of the first page the name, Sir Walter Wingate, caught his attention. His eyes narrowed as he continued to read and by the time he had finished he was scowling.

"Now what the devil caused Captain Jones to write such a thing?" he uttered. He reread the letter slowly.

"We are moored next to Sir Walter Wingate's ketch, although something one of my friends said makes me slightly apprehensive and I'm endeavoring to find a safer anchorage. It appears that this ketch has the worst crew, slovenly and offensive. Not that I mind their manners, for I don't have to give them the time of day. It's the night voyages they have been taking recently that concern me, for if the crew do not know that much about sailing, there is no saying that we won't get hit broadside."

Lord Romford folded the letter in two and put it into the top drawer of his desk. "I wonder what it all means. The good captain doesn't say anything appears suspicious . . . yet . . ." He paused in his reflections as he endeavored to make sense of this latest piece of news. He shook his head in annoyance. There were simply too many loose ends which made it impossible to reach any logical conclusion. He strode over to the bellrope and tugged it hard. Minutes later the butler appeared and after asking him to send Felix in, he moved to the window.

His study, on the south side of the house, looked out onto the rose gardens and as he waited for Felix to join him, he allowed his gaze to wander over his land. It was a refreshing sight, the flowers in the foreground a perfect complement to the golden fields behind. He smiled as he saw Miranda walk toward the flower beds, scissors and basket in hand. Without her bonnet on, her hair glinted in the sun and she seemed to be singing, for he could see her lips moving. For a moment he was tempted to join her and was about to open the French windows when Felix walked in.

"I was just coming in search of you, Hugo, when I heard you wanted to see me. What really happened in London?"

Reluctantly, Lord Romford turned back into the room. "It was as I said, Felix. Nothing. I have left my agent in charge of tracking down the dealer who bought the paintings and I hope to hear from him soon. Can you tell me what has caused Anita's misery? I have never seen her in such a depression of spirits."

"I haven't noticed anything amiss, but then I haven't spent too much time here. She seems perfectly all right to me. It's Miranda I'm concerned about, Hugo, for I have learnt some distressing facts about Rodney and, frankly, I don't think you should encourage him in his pursuit of her. There's something havey-cavey about his movements that makes me believe he was involved in the theft of your pictures."

Lord Romford raised his eyebrows and caressed his chin with his hand thoughtfully. "Tell me what it is that you have uncovered," he said at length, and then listened closely to what Felix had to say. "Very interesting," he remarked, when Felix had finished, "very interesting indeed. Have either you or Miranda asked Rodney if this is so?"

"No. Miranda said it was best to wait for you to return. Anyway, she thinks Rodney will have a perfectly reasonable explanation."

"I'm not so sure about that. You see, I'm bothered by Rodney's failure to mention that I have three reproductions reposing in my art gallery. He's an expert and must have noticed. Now this suggestion that he was seen with Roberts the day before the man died. And, on top of all that, I have just learnt that Walter keeps a yacht in Newport and has taken to sailing at night."

"Hmm," Felix commented, unconsciously imitating his brother's gesture of stroking his chin. "It doesn't look good, does it? Roberts must have been killed because he knew too much."

"The question now is, who killed him? I can't believe Rodney capable of such an act, but . . ." Lord Romford's voice trailed off and a troubled expression crossed his face.

"But what, Hugo?"

"When a man is desperate, there's no telling what he'll do. Who's to say that Rodney didn't deliberately engineer the whole scene at Vauxhall just to gain unlimited access to this house?"

"How could he have been certain that you would send Miranda here?" Felix asked.

"I've thought about that," Lord Romford replied, and then snapped his fingers. "I do believe I'm the one that's been duped. The morning after that episode I called in at White's and met with Rodney. It was at his suggestion that I sent Miranda here. He said it would give him the opportunity to woo her, and, dammit, Felix, I went along with it because I really believed him."

Felix stared at his brother in horror. "Do you think Miranda is in any danger?"

"I don't know, but it's unlikely. However, I think it high time I talked with her and told her she can break with Rodney. You see, when I spoke to him this morning, I didn't know of this development. I even hinted to him that I wouldn't hold him to the engagement. He refused the offer, but in such a way that convinced me he doesn't love her at all."

A noise at the window caused them both to turn and Lord Romford was forced to smile as he saw Miranda, her face pressed against a pane, distorting the shape into ugliness. "Leave me alone with her, Felix," he said softly as he walked toward the glass doors. "I don't think she would appreciate your presence while we discuss Rodney."

Felix nodded and by the time Lord Romford had opened the doors he had left the room.

Eleven

Miranda, regretting her earlier promise to Anita to cut some flowers after lunch, had tried to delay the chore, but Anita wouldn't hear of it.

"It won't take you long," she said, "and I need them for the sitting room. The arrangement in there is a positive disgrace."

"It's been like that all morning, another hour won't hurt. After all, it's not as though we were expecting visitors," Miranda said. She was consumed with curiosity to find out what her guardian had really discovered on his trip to London. She certainly didn't believe he had meant what he had said.

"Away with you, Miranda, before I lose my temper," Anita retorted sharply. "And don't forget I want mostly blues and pinks."

"Oh, very well," Miranda said gracelessly and, picking up a basket, departed. Her ill-humor evaporated once she was outside, though, and she immediately regretted her churlishness toward Anita. "I'm a fool," she muttered. "I should realize that poor Anita isn't herself. If we don't solve this mystery and prove Rodney's innocence, I'm afraid she will go into a decline and it will be all my fault. But I can't call the engagement off," she continued, talking to a rosebud, "for if I do, then Rodney will be free to declare himself to her." She snipped the bud and laid it carefully in the basket looped over her arm. "Oh, dear, who ever would have thought love could be so complicated." Shrugging, she worked swiftly and soon her basket was overflowing with a variety of blooms.

On an impulse she walked across the terrace toward Lord Romford's study. Inside she could see that he was in deep conversation with Felix. Feeling annoyed that once again she was being excluded, she hurried to the windows. Pressing her face against the pane, she tapped on the glass to attract their attention.

Lord Romford's smile as he turned and saw her made her laugh. He looked extraordinarily handsome in his close-fitting riding clothes. As she waited for him to open the doors it suddenly occurred to her that someday he would marry and she would no longer be welcome in his home. "Silly girl," she told herself fiercely, and stuck her tongue out to give herself courage.

"What a face," Lord Romford laughed as he unlocked the doors. "If the wind changes, you'll be stuck like that."

"An old wives' tale," she responded airily but quickly pulled herself away from the glass and stepped inside. "Where is Felix? I thought I saw him here."

"You frightened him away," Lord Romford replied casually. "Here, let me take your basket and sit down. I want to talk to you."

She stood at the threshold for a moment and looked up at him. Their eyes met and she had the strangest notion that she was seeing him for the first time. "That sounds ominous. Have you two been conspiring against me?" Her voice sounded unnaturally high to her. She was shaken by what had just transpired and bewildered by the intensity of feeling she had just experienced. "If you have," she continued in a shaky voice, "I won't forgive either of you."

"There's nothing to forgive," he replied, his tone grave. If he was aware of the turmoil raging within his ward's breast, he gave no hint of it. "Felix has been telling me about his trip to Tintern. Miranda, I want you to call off the engagement."

Miranda shook her head defiantly. "I don't want to . . . now."

"You mean you have grown fond of Rodney?" Lord Romford asked in amazement.

Miserably aware that she was trapped, she was forced to nod. "I don't care what Felix has heard, I don't believe Rodney is capable of such intrigue and I have every intention of standing by him."

Lord Romford looked stunned at this display of loyalty. It was the last thing he had expected. "I hope you will forgive me if I say you are allowing your loyalty for an old friend to sway your emotions." His voice was cold. "Do you really believe that you love Rodney enough to marry him if he was involved with Roberts's death?"

"We don't know that he was," Miranda said, ignoring his question. "What do you want of me? If you recall, it was at your insistence that I came down here to get better acquainted with him. Now, having done that and finding myself perfectly content to let the engagement stand, you order me to end it. Well, I won't do it, and that's final." Her initial show of temper had been forced, but now, as she finished speaking, she really did feel angry. "You have no more consideration of my feelings than . . . than . . . that bellrope over there," she continued hotly. "You seem to think that I can be pushed and pulled in any direction to accommodate your every whim. But not this time, Hugo, and nothing you say will make me change my mind."

"I hope you know what you are doing, then, Miranda," he replied in clipped tone. It was obvious that her outburst had infuriated him and as she watched him struggling to control himself she was unable to resist one last thrust.

"If the day should ever dawn when you find yourself in love, maybe you will understand how I feel." She lifted her head high and stalked out of the study. "That will teach him," she said angrily as she mounted the stairs. It was only when she reached her room and her fury had abated that she realized she had allowed her temper to complicate matters even more. Throwing herself on her bed she gave way to the misery that enveloped her and for the next ten minutes indulged herself in a satisfying bout of tears.

Pleading a headache, she stayed in her chamber for the rest of the afternoon. However, just before dinner, Anita came to see how she was and tried to persuade her to go downstairs.

"I . . . I . . . don't feel up to it," Miranda replied wearily. "I don't think I could face Hugo tonight. I might just lose my temper again and that would only upset you."

Anita stroked her arm in a sympathetic gesture. "Poor, poor Miranda," she said. "It does seem that you two cannot be left alone without quarreling. Hugo is pacing the library with such a black look on his face that even Felix is steering well clear of him. What on earth did you two find to argue about this time?"

"His high-handed ways, if I recall correctly," Miranda answered. "Honestly, Anita, he treats me like he would a piece of furniture. Something that should be dusted off and polished up and then shrouded in holland covers until the next time it's to be used."

"Don't you think you're being slightly irrational?" Anita queried quietly. "I know Hugo is somewhat overbearing at times, but then you are not as thoughtful as you could be. The sad truth is that you are both too volatile to be at peace with each other for more than a few minutes at a stretch. Why don't you get yourself ready and come on downstairs? We can't have you two on the outs for tomorrow, otherwise we'll have to cancel the hunt."

"I'm not hungry," Miranda said. She spoke the truth, for the idea of having to face Lord Romford had chased her appetite away. He would never understand why she had spoken as she had and she was afraid that this time she had pushed him too far. Why, oh, why couldn't he have told her to break the engagement before he went to London?

"Sulking isn't going to do you any good either," Anita said with a touch of exasperation. "You are no longer a schoolgirl, Miranda, but a young lady on the threshold of womanhood, and I beseech you to act like one."

"Please don't make me any more miserable than I am," Miranda countered in a small voice. "I do my best to behave, but . . . but sometimes . . . Oh! I don't know, sometimes Hugo makes it impossible." She could feel the tears gathering in her eyes again and brushed them away impatiently.

"There, there, child," Anita soothed. "I didn't mean to cause you more pain. I won't press you." She made as though to leave the room, shaking her head at her failure.

Impulsively, Miranda turned and detained her. There was something to the sad set of Anita's shoulders that made it impossible for her to refuse the request. "I'll come down, Anita," she said, forcing herself to speak lightly. "And I promise I'll apologize to Hugo."

Anita smiled at her, evidently pleased that her charge had decided to be reasonable. "I'd best go down and tell chef to put back the dinner by half an hour. That should give you plenty of time."

It was with great trepidation that Miranda descended the stairs some time later and knocked on the library door. Normally, she would have entered without that formality, but the apprehension she felt made her want to delay the inevitable confrontation. When she heard the stern voice of Lord Romford bid her enter, she opened the door slowly and poked her head in. "Do you have a few moments, Hugo?" she asked hesitantly. The black scowl on his face almost made her withdraw.

He nodded. "I'm glad to see that you have recovered from your indisposition," he said stiffly.

Refusing to let his attitude deter her, she walked across the room until she was standing in front of him. "I merely came to apologize, Hugo, and to make amends." She touched his arm as she spoke, her first, tentative gesture of peace. "We can hardly be at odds with each other living under the same roof, can we?"

A reluctant smile played across his face, erasing all traces of his earlier scowl. "You're a beguiling little witch, young lady," he said, tweaking a tendril of her hair. "You make it impossible for me to be out of sorts with you for long, no matter how incorrigible you have been."

Once again, Miranda was aware of a strange sensation coursing through her body and, thinking it to be because of his careless caress, pulled away. "I won't change my mind about Rodney, though," she said honestly. "But we needn't let that interfere with our trying to solve the mystery, need we?"

A look of annoyance sprang into his eyes, but he merely shook his head. "Stubborn to the end," he said in a carefully controlled voice, "but I agree to keep the truce. However, there are certain things you should be aware of, Miranda, though I don't think this is an appropriate time to speak of them."

"You . . . you came across more, damaging information in London?" she asked warily.

"Not about Rodney," he responded truthfully. "I did discover that my three pictures have been sold to a questionable dealer and my agent is now trying to discover who sold them. And then, quite unrelated to that, Captain Jones tells me that Walter keeps a yacht at Newport."

"Is that so very odd?"

"No, but apparently the boat has been out on a few mysterious night sailings lately, and I would dearly love to know what they were all about."

"Could Captain Jones find out? It would be easy enough for him to fall into conversation with a crew member."

Lord Romford smiled at her again. "The clarity of your reasoning is a constant delight, Miranda, for that is precisely what I have suggested to him."

Miranda felt a warm glow at this praise. "Felix told you of the second passage?" she asked.

"Indeed, and I think I shall have it blocked up again."

"Oh! No, Hugo. Just think, if Walter knows of its existence and decides to use it, we'll be able to catch him. Please don't, not yet awhile," she appealed.

Lord Romford, as though anxious not to cause another rift, reluctantly agreed. "I'll delay it for a week. If we haven't discovered the truth by then, the passageway to your bedroom will be closed and I shall ask Dr. Thompson to reopen the whole matter."

Miranda, equally anxious not to jeopardize their newfound harmony, nodded and said lightly, "With your brains and my beauty I'm sure we'll come up with the solution." The dinner gong drowned out the rest of her words and she hooked her arm into her guardian's and they proceeded to the dining room, both well pleased with themselves.

Anita was happy to see that her cousin had regained his good humor and said as much. Felix, who had been aware of the disagreement and that he had been the primary cause of it, was nonetheless puzzled by Miranda's attitude toward the viscount, for she had certainly not confided in him her sudden change of feelings. However, thinking that his brother had enough to contend with, he refrained from making any comment, vowing instead to keep an eye on her. He suspected she was up to something but, quite what, was beyond his comprehension.

After dinner, Miranda excused herself in order to lay the false trail, should it be needed. When she had finished she went in search of Felix. Anita informed her that both he and Lord Romford had ridden over to the squire's for some card playing and after a half hour of idle chitchat, both ladies retired to bed.

The next morning Miranda was downstairs early. She felt excited and apprehensive. What if Sir Walter exposed his hand? she wondered. Would they be prepared? With this idea in mind she decided to arm herself and took herself to the gun room. She was a little out of practice, not having handled a pistol since her brother's death, but this fact didn't deter her in the slightest. She had been well taught by Justin and knew that her aim would be deadly accurate if the worst happened.

The gun room was small, but adequately stocked. Lord Romford wasn't a great believer in the use of firearms.

"They can be dangerous," he had said, "if they get into the hands of nervous people." And when Miranda had asked him how he would defend himself if it were necessary, he had patted a sword. "This is my weapon and it can be just as deadly as any gun. Moreover, it's not subject to the vagaries of explosives."

Now she stood in the doorway for a few moments, surveying the three glass-fronted cupboards the room housed, before moving toward the one containing the dueling pistols. She opened the door and carefully took out the smallest box. Placing it on a table that sat in the middle of the room, she lifted the lid and smiled at what she saw. Two perfectly matched ivory-handled weapons stared up at her, small enough to be concealed in the pocket of her dress. She took one of them out and weighed it in her hand. It was light and easy to handle, just right for a woman. Working quickly, she lifted her arm and aimed the gun at the window. She pulled the trigger slowly and, satisfied with the action, primed the weapon, ensuring that the safety catch was down before slipping it into her pocket.

"At least I'll be prepared," she murmured as she removed all traces of her presence. "I only hope I won't have to use it."

Closing the door behind her, she hurried to the sitting room, where she found Anita sitting on a coach nervously pulling at some tangled silks.

"Here, let me help you," she said, "although I don't know why you're bothering with them. Rodney and Sir Walter will be here shortly and we can begin our hunt."

"I . . . I was thinking that perhaps I wouldn't join in," Anita began, but Miranda, knowing her hesitancy was due to her desire to avoid the viscount, quickly put an end to this suggestion.

"I simply won't allow such poor spirits," she said firmly. "I'm relying on your quick wits to make this morning a success. You know full well that Felix is harebrained, Sir Walter is not overly enthusiastic, and Rodney and Hugo consider themselves far too old to indulge in such childish amusement."

"Surely you can get by without me," Anita responded miserably. "I'm afraid that my ill-humor will only put a pall on the whole proceedings."

Miranda was about to deny this, when the butler entered to announce the arrival of the viscount and Sir Walter. So, instead, she grinned at Anita and whispered, "It's too late now to cry off," before turning to greet the visitors.

Minutes later, Lord Romford joined them and suggested some refreshment, "to sustain us for the ordeal ahead. And Felix has been detained, but he should be with us shortly."

Miranda shot her guardian a quizzical look, but Lord Romford declined to enlarge further on his brother's absence. His attitude toward the viscount was cool and in an effort to put everyone at ease, Miranda launched into an explanation of the approaching activities.

"We're really trying to find the ring," she said. "Felix has discovered a secret passageway and we thought to search it thoroughly in case the ring is hidden in a recess."

"You mean you've known of its existence and haven't combed every nook and cranny?" Sir Walter drawled sarcastically. His eyes narrowed menacingly as he spoke and for a moment Miranda felt afraid.

She gave a little laugh as she shook her head. "But that wouldn't be fair," she answered. "We only took the most cursory glances and there were so many cobwebs I vowed I wouldn't return until the passageway had been cleared."

"I do hope there aren't any animals," Anita interposed faintly. "I . . . I don't think I could bear to feel anything brushing up against my feet."

"We've plenty of men to protect us," Miranda reassured her, "but I think your fears are needless, for Felix said the ground bore no tracks. . . " She paused before adding, ". . . of animals, that is." She sensed rather than saw Sir Walter stiffen at this, and avoided looking at him. *Let him wonder what I mean,* she thought fiercely. *I'll prove that I'm not so easily intimidated.* "Anyway, Anita," she continued, "we'll have candles to light our way."

"I'll walk in front of you," the viscount murmured to Anita, "so don't worry."

Obviously embarrassed by his show of concern, Anita lapsed into silence and continued to unravel her silks in a distracted manner.

"All is not lost," Miranda said, "for if we fail to locate the ring I have provided alternative amusements."

"What are they?" the viscount asked gallantly. "The specter of the Welsh lady to guide us to the resting place of the coins?"

Miranda giggled. "No, but I do wish I had thought of it. What a scare I would have given you all."

"Then I, for one, am certainly grateful that your imagination failed you on this occasion," Anita said faintly. "Specters indeed!"

The conversation came to a halt as the refreshments and Felix arrived simultaneously. Dismissing the butler, Anita moved over to the tray and poured two glasses of lemonade for herself and Miranda. Sir Walter followed her and asked softly if he could help.

Surprised by this friendly overture, Anita nodded. "By all means. If you could inquire of the gentlemen what it is they require, and this is for Miranda." She handed him a glass and watched him briefly until Felix claimed her attention.

"I'm famished," he exclaimed. "What do we have in the way of food?"

Anita looked down at the array of plates before her. "I'm afraid I can offer little to assuage your appetite. Butterfly cakes, buttered scones, or"—she bent down to inspect the third plate more closely —"or macaroons." She picked up the plate and proffered it to Felix. "Try them, they're delicious."

Felix shook his head. "Thank you, but no thank you. I'll just nip down to the kitchens and see if there are any pies. Macaroons aren't my style."

"Not dignified enough for you?" Anita teased.

"Well, now that you mention it, they are a bit too dainty. Not only that, I don't think they would taste so good with ale."

"In that case," Anita laughed, "have a glass of lemonade."

Felix's response was to pull a face. "Excuse me while I go in search of that pie. My mouth is already watering at the thought of it." However, before he had time to move, Lord Romford's voice cut in.

"Ladies and gentlemen," he announced in loud tones, "I think it is time we started to hunt for the treasure. As Miranda has already informed you, a secret passageway has been discovered, an entrance of which is located in the gallery." He surveyed the group in front of him and smiled mechanically. "Shall we proceed?"

Miranda, anxious to escape from Sir Walter's side, was the first to move. She put down her half-finished drink and hurried to the door. Suddenly the room seemed to spin in front of her and she could feel beads of perspiration forming on her forehead. She shook her head in an effort to clear it, grasping the door knob for support. She was vaguely aware of Sir Walter moving out of her line of vision and she looked round wildly for Lord Romford. Something was wrong. Very wrong. She couldn't see properly, everything was blurred. "I . . . I . . . please, I don't feel well," she whispered. "My head . . . my eyes . . . " She could feel herself falling, but somehow her guardian reached her side

before she reached the floor. He grasped her about
the waist and led her to a chair. "Sit down, Miranda," he urged gently, "and put your head between
your knees."

With a supreme effort she fought off the waves
of nausea and did as Lord Romford suggested. She
was aware of the others crowding about and Lord
Romford commanding Felix to open a window, yet
it all seemed to be happening at a distance.

"What do you think is the matter?" she heard
the viscount ask. He sounded anxious.

"Too much excitement and too little food," Anita
replied practically. "In the last two days she's eaten
very little."

Miranda struggled to sit up, but the pressure of
Lord Romford's hand on her shoulder forced her
down again. "I'll . . . I'll be all right in a minute,"
she mumbled. "If . . . if I could just get some fresh
air. . . ."

"I think the best place for you, my girl," Lord
Romford said calmly, "is bed. Anita, be so good as
to ask Mrs. Lloyd to prepare some strong, sweet tea
and then meet me in Miranda's bedroom." He bent
down and with great ease scooped Miranda up into
his arms. She leaned back against him, too weak to
fight. She felt wretched. "I'm afraid we'll have to
postpone the hunt," he continued, and walked from
the room.

"I'll be fine in a moment," Miranda protested
feebly. "Please don't cancel it."

"Having waited this long, I think we can wait
another day or two," Lord Romford said firmly.
"What you are in need of is some rest and nourish-
ment."

He mounted the stairs quickly, carrying his
charge easily. She opened her eyes and squinted up

at him. Her vision had cleared a little and she could see the look of concern on his face. *It is reassuring to know he is near at hand to protect me,* she thought. Shifting slightly in his arms, she nestled her head into the hollow of his shoulder and a small sigh escaped her.

"Feeling better?" Lord Romford asked as he tightened his hold on her.

Miranda nodded dreamily. The dizziness had passed, but she still felt light-headed. "I think I can walk now," she said and then immediately regretted saying that as Lord Romford released her, for she suddenly realized she had enjoyed being in his arms. Blushing slightly at the turn her thoughts had taken, she walked slowly toward her bedroom.

"Miranda," Lord Romford said, "do you think Sir Walter put something into your drink? Stupidly, I wasn't watching him when he carried your lemonade over."

"I . . . I don't know, Hugo," she answered. "It's possible, but what could his motive have been?"

Lord Romford shrugged his shoulders. "Maybe to postpone the hunt in order to give himself time to find the coins. . . ."

". . . He doesn't know we have the ring," Miranda interrupted.

Lord Romford looked thoughtful for a moment. "In that case, I believe it's high time we let him know."

"Oh! But you must wait for me to be present before you do," Miranda protested. "You and Felix are having all the fun, while I'm left to languish in ignorance."

Her guardian greeted this remark with a deep chuckle, his amusement at her choice of words apparent. "I promise I won't do anything until you have recovered," he said. "Now, off to bed with you and get some rest."

Warmed by his words, Miranda smiled. "Please tell Anita I don't want the tea," she said and closed the bedroom door behind her. Within minutes she was fast asleep.

Twelve

By the time Lord Romford returned to the gallery, the visitors had departed.

"Rodney said he would ride over this afternoon to inquire after Miranda's health," Anita remarked, "and . . . and if you don't need me for anything I'll go and see if she is comfortable before I have a rest myself."

Lord Romford put a restraining hand on her arm. "Let her be, Anita. I think your observation was correct. All she needs is sleep." For a moment he was tempted to tell her what was really happening and seek her advice, but something held him back. Instead, he smiled at her reassuringly and said that Miranda would be down later.

"It's quite obvious," he said to Felix later, "that Anita has formed a tendre for Rodney. I noticed how studiously she ignored him this morning. And a few days ago she informed me she wanted to return to her sister."

"Anita and Rodney!" Felix laughed. "I think you have been smitten with Miranda's disease and are allowing your imagination too much leeway."

Lord Romford refrained from further comment as he deftly shuffled a pack of cards with one hand. They were seated at a table in the library, the ring on the table between them, once again playing around with the theory that the cards their ancestor had in his hand were of significance. "I hope you are right, Felix," he commented finally, "for it would give me no satisfaction to see Anita breaking her heart over a scoundrel."

"The thing I don't understand is why Miranda is being so obstinate about sticking with the engagement. She must have her reasons, but I'm damned if I know what they are. Thank goodness I don't have to marry and produce an heir. I swear, the idea of being tied to one woman for the rest of my life isn't an enjoyable thought."

Lord Romford laughed. "Are you trying to tell me it's about time I settled down?" he inquired.

"Good heavens, no!" Felix exclaimed. "Wouldn't dream of telling you how to run your life, Hugo." He paused thoughtfully for a moment as though struck by a strange notion. "Thing is, I suppose you will have to one day, won't you?"

"One day," Lord Romford agreed with a smile. It was a sobering thought and one he didn't want to pursue. "Do you want to sort the cards?" he asked of his brother as he casually picked up the ring. "I believe the old man was holding the eight of hearts, the nine and Jack of clubs, and the ten of diamonds."

Felix proceeded to pull out the cards from the deck and placed them in front of him.

"I told Miranda that I think the time has come to force Walter's hand," Lord Romford said. "Should the opportunity present itself, I'm going to tell him we've found the ring."

"A good idea," Felix responded enthusiastically. "I think we have gotten ourselves into a corner and playing around with these cards isn't helping a bit. I'm convinced they were only painted in to confuse the issue. We need some action."

Lord Romford put the ring down and fingered the cards. As he pulled them toward him, his lace cuff caught the ring and sent it spinning to the floor. Both men heard a faint click and as Felix bent down to retrieve it, he saw the face of it had opened.

"Look at this, Hugo," Felix said excitedly. "That fall has set off a spring." As he straightened up he looked at the cavity and saw it was empty. "Whatever was in it has gone," he observed as he handed it to his brother.

"And Roberts must have found it," Lord Romford commented.

"Of course," Felix agreed, snapping his fingers. "His last words must have been the clue that was concealed in the ring." He scratched his head. "It still doesn't make sense, though, does it?"

"No, dammit," Lord Romford said crossly. "I have a feeling that the solution is so simple, yet it has me baffled even now." He tossed the object of his anger on the table and rose from his seat. "It's not that I care about finding the coins, it's the knowledge that our ancestor is sitting up 'there,' " he said, pointing to the ceiling, "laughing at our stupidity that irks me." He walked to the door. "Come, let's go for a ride and clear our heads, for it is apparent we aren't going to accomplish anything sitting here. I only hope that I hear from my agent soon. I told him to put up in Tintern and send word to me when he arrives. I don't want Rodney seeing him, at least not yet awhile." He stalked out and Felix hurried after him.

When Miranda awoke, she felt much better. Her head had cleared and the strange feeling in the pit of her stomach had vanished. In fact, she felt very hungry. She bent down to pick up her dress and as she did so, the gun fell out of the pocket and dropped, with a clatter, to the ground. A little smile played across her lips as she picked it up. Her earlier action of arming herself now seemed melodramatic. Sir Walter was perfectly capable of getting what he wanted without resorting to violence. But the face of Anthony Roberts flashed before her and she shuddered. If Sir Walter was responsible for that death, then he was also capable of extreme violence. With this in mind, she hid the pistol under her pillow before dressing.

The heavy silence that greeted her as she descended the stairs indicated that no one was at home and so she was surprised to hear the muted sound of voices as she passed the sitting room. She hesitated before opening the door, looking round for the footman. His post was deserted, though, and she frowned. She had no desire to see the viscount or Sir Walter if, indeed, they were still here, yet the absence of the footman denied her the privilege of inquiring who the visitors were. In the end, her curiosity overcame her reluctance and she opened the door.

The sight before her held her spellbound for several seconds and then she let out an involuntary gasp. There, locked in a tender embrace, were Anita and the viscount.

Her gasp caused the lovers to break apart. In the confusion that followed, Miranda managed to hide her dismay under a benevolent smile. Anita, her handkerchief pressed to her face, struggled to apologize and the viscount stood in front of her, as though protecting her.

"I . . . I . . . am at a loss to know what to say," he began, his voice quivering with emotion. "What you just witnessed, Miranda, wasn't . . . wasn't. . ."

"Oh! Rodney," Miranda interrupted quickly, "you've done exactly the right thing . . . at least I hope you have."

Anita looked at the viscount in astonishment, obviously not believing what she had just heard.

"I . . . I'm appalled by my display of manners," the viscount continued. "Indeed, I . . . " He broke off as he suddenly realized what Miranda had said. "What did you say?" he asked, now as bewildered as Anita. "The right thing?"

"I knew you were in love with Anita an age ago, Rodney, only I was hoping that I could keep you tied to my side a while longer. . . ." She paused in order to give herself time to think. She could hardly give them the real reason for her actions. She would have to confide in Anita later, she owed her that, but now she had to find an excuse that would explain why she wasn't enacting a Cheltenham tragedy over her fiancé's faithless behavior.

"You . . . you knew?" Anita queried softly. "I . . . I had kept my feelings to myself. Can you ever forgive me, Miranda?"

Grateful for the interruption, Miranda nodded. "Dearest Anita, there is nothing to forgive. I would like to wish you well, and tell you both how delighted I am, for I most truly am. I . . . I . . . have but one stipulation to make, though. I want you to keep your love for each other a secret for the time being. I can't give you the reason at the moment, but . . . but it's important that Hugo thinks me engaged to you, Rodney."

The viscount looked at Anita tenderly, before turning his attention to Miranda. "I'm reluctant to practice such a deceit, for it will be one difficult to maintain. My purpose in calling here this afternoon was to inquire after your welfare, not to seduce Anita. But, finding her alone and in tears, my control snapped and, but for your understanding, would have compromised her shamefully."

"You must try, Rodney," Miranda said with some impatience. "It will simply never do for Hugo to discover your secret at the moment."

Anita laid her hand on the viscount's arm. "Rodney, my love," she whispered, "I think I know Miranda's reason for asking us to do this, and I . . . I would like to agree. It won't be for long, I promise."

Miranda tried to conceal her dismay at these words. Had Rodney told Anita of his involvement with Roberts? she wondered. She dismissed the idea, knowing that it couldn't be so. Anita would never condone such behavior, no matter how much she loved him.

The viscount, looking far from happy, agreed reluctantly to this scheme. "I hope that you will release me from this promise in the very near future," he added, "for I cannot like misleading my friends. There has been too much of that already." He turned away, afraid that he had said too much, and began pacing the room.

Anita, the happiness she felt shining from her

eyes, reassured him that the wait wouldn't be of a long duration. "Trust me, Rodney," she said, "I know everything will work out."

The viscount let out a frustrated groan and gathered Anita into the shelter of his arms. "You try a man's patience sorely," he murmured against her sweet-smelling hair, "but you have my word."

Miranda, slightly embarrassed by this open display of affection, withdrew to the windows. Rodney's statement about too many people being misled was puzzling, and surely indicated that he was innocent of any crime. She believed in his integrity, no matter what Hugo and Felix had discovered. Suddenly, all her misgivings about the inadvisability of his declaring himself at such an inopportune moment vanished and she felt much better as she rejoined the lovers.

The viscount took his departure shortly after and Anita, overcome by the events of the afternoon, burst into tears. "Miranda, Miranda," she sobbed, "if I didn't think you had acted out of the best of motives, I would scold you. I have been so miserable this last week thinking that . . . that you had finally fallen in love with Rodney. Why, I almost returned to my sister."

Miranda had the grace to look guilty. "I'm sorry, Anita, really I am. My intentions were well meant."

"I can see now that you sought to catch Hugo's interest," Anita continued, as she dried her eyes.

"I did what?" Miranda gasped. This suggestion sounded so ridiculous she couldn't help but laugh.

Confused, Anita looked at her charge. "I . . . I . . . but that's why I persuaded Rodney to keep our love for each other a secret. To . . . to give you time to make Hugo jealous." She broke off, flustered by the mirth Miranda was displaying.

"Oh! Anita, Anita," she giggled, holding her sides in an effort to control herself. "What a romantic you have turned into. Mr. Horace Bateman would be well pleased with you."

"Then what *is* your reason?" Anita quizzed, determined not to be sidetracked.

A sober look settled on Miranda's face and she sat down. "Sit down as well, Anita," she said, "for I think the time has arrived when I'm going to have to tell you everything."

Anita obeyed, Miranda's serious tone chasing away her buoyancy. "What is it, Miranda? Are you really in love with Rodney?"

"No, no," Miranda replied hastily. "It is quite another matter entirely, one that stems from Anthony Roberts's death." She told the story slowly, omitting nothing. When she reached the point in her tale of the viscount's possible involvement, Anita turned ashen and clutched at the fringes of her shawl nervously.

"I don't believe it," she managed, her voice shaking. "Rodney wouldn't be implicated in such things. It's impossible, absolutely impossible."

"I agree with you, Anita, but don't you see how odd his actions have been? I think he knows that Walter is involved, at least in stealing the paintings, and is trying to sort the whole affair out with the least possible embarrassment to all concerned."

"It has to be," Anita stated with conviction. "It has to be. Only, I wish he would confide in Hugo."

"So you see, Anita," Miranda continued, "I was trying to keep up the pretense of my engagement to Rodney until his innocence had been established. I . . . I . . . didn't want you to be upset."

"Dear child, thank you, but I'm glad that I know. It explains many things."

"I have to ask you not to mention anything to
Rodney just yet, Anita. Indeed, perhaps it would be
best if nobody knew you knew. . . . I mean Hugo
and Felix as well. It might prove awkward and they
will surely ask why I told you."

Anita sat meditating on this, and Miranda let
her be. She was glad that everything was now out
in the open, for it had become exceedingly difficult
to keep Anita in ignorance of the true state of
affairs. A few times recently she had almost let
something slip in Anita's presence that would have
aroused her suspicions.

"About that ring," Anita said at length. "Did you
say the face resembles a queen?"

"I'm sorry, Anita, what did you say?" Miranda
asked, and when Anita repeated her question, she
nodded her head. "Yes, and Roberts's last words
were, 'The queen makes the flush.' "

"What surprises me is that Hugo has not
tumbled to the answer," Anita said serenely. "The
solution is quite obvious to me."

Miranda jumped up excitedly. "How can you sit
there so calmly and make a pronouncement like
that? What is the answer?"

"One of the bedrooms, in fact the one you are
occupying, is called the queen's boudoir. Apparently Princess Elizabeth spent the night there before
she ascended to the throne."

"She did!" Miranda exclaimed in astonishment.
"In my bedroom. I am honored. I can't understand
why Hugo failed to mention it, for he must know
that I would be pleased by such information."

"I read about it in one of the books in the library.
I suppose it's possible that Hugo doesn't know of it.
Indeed, I'm persuaded he cannot, else he would
have made the connection immediately."

It was Miranda's turn to look thoughtful. If she could get hold of the ring, without Lord Romford's knowledge, and take it to her room, maybe she could find the hidden coins. She felt a surge of excitement.

Anita, worried by her silence, broke into her thoughts. "You will tell Hugo, won't you, Miranda?" she asked, concerned lest Miranda keep this information to herself.

"Of course, Anita," Miranda lied. "Of course." Shortly after, she excused herself on the pretext of going to the kitchens. Instead, she hurried to Lord Romford's study. She knew he kept the ring in his desk drawer. However, she discovered the drawer was empty. She swore in a most unladylike manner. "I wonder what he has done with it?" she murmured and, after a moment's consideration, clicked her fingers. "Of course, I expect he has left it out somewhere so that Sir Walter can see it if he calls." She gave a cursory glance about the study and then took herself off to the library. The cards and ring were still on the table and with a pleased laugh she quickly pocketed the ring. "I think I shall retire to my room now," she observed to her reflection that stared up from the glass-topped table, "and use my indisposition as an excuse not to come down for dinner."

Feigning a headache, she rejoined Anita and set her plan into motion.

"You do look a little peaked," Anita agreed sympathetically. "Indeed, with all the excitement, I feel somewhat under par. I think I shall follow your example and have my dinner on a tray in my room."

This piece of news delighted Miranda, for it meant that Anita wouldn't remind her to relay the legend of the queen's boudoir to Hugo until the morning. And, with luck, she might well have found the coins. "That's an excellent idea," she agreed. "I swear you are enveloped in a golden aura of love that is bound to arouse the suspicions of even the greatest cynic."

Anita blushed and smiled. "It would be difficult for me to behave with any degree of normalcy," she confessed. "I feel as though I'm floating on air."

"I'm so pleased for you, Anita," Miranda said impulsively. "I do hope that I will fall in love one day. It must be a most comfortable feeling."

"Comfortable!" Anita exclaimed. "I haven't known a moment's peace since I met Rodney. There's nothing comfortable about love, Miranda. It's. . . it's . . . quite awesome really. At least I find it so."

"But you are happy?" Miranda pressed.

"Indubitably, but frightened nonetheless. Come, let us retire before Hugo and Felix return. All this chatter of romance has made me quite dizzy."

The two of them ascended the stairs, arm in arm, laughing over some remark of Anita's.

Once in the privacy of her own room, however, Miranda's good spirits deserted her as she pondered her lonely state. Not even the thought of finding the coins consoled her.

Thirteen

The swirling, gray mist enfolded Lord Romford and Felix as they guided their horses carefully down the mountain. They were on their way home from Tintern, having spent a pleasant afternoon looking at some horses that were for sale.

"Damned weather," Felix muttered. "One minute we are basking in the sunshine and the next being soaked to the skin. What a wretched country Wales is."

"If you knew how to behave," Lord Romford remarked dryly, "you would be enjoying the climate Oxford offers. Personally, I like the daily inconsistencies of the weather here."

"I always thought you a little touched in the upper works," Felix said with affectionate disregard for his brother's rank. "I refuse to believe that anyone can enjoy daily inconsistencies. Far too inconvenient."

Lord Romford laughed. "Where's your spirit of adventure, Felix? You mustn't become so set in your ways, else you'll be old before your time."

Felix snorted his disagreement of this prophecy. "Hardly, old boy," he responded, carefully emphasizing the word old. "If I keep your company, I'm more likely to catch a cold and die young." He reined in his horse and looked about him. "I fail to understand what you find so attractive about this. I can barely see five feet ahead of me, the damp has ruined my hessians, and we're miles from the nearest tavern, which means that I will have to contend with my thirst until we return to Ramsden."

"The mist will lift soon," Lord Romford reassured him. "Your boots, if you give them to Watkins, will be returned to you in perfect condition, and if you take a sip out of this, I daresay your thirst will be quenched." As he spoke he handed Felix a hip flask. "Now, shall we proceed? I want to let Miranda know that we have told Walter about the ring before he gives her the news first. Otherwise she will accuse us of keeping her in the dark again."

"And knowing Walter, he will not waste a moment before trying to get his hands on the trinket."

Lord Romford rode on in thoughtful silence. He was bothered by many aspects of the puzzle still confronting him, but what concerned him more was Miranda's attitude and her refusal to break off the engagement. It was as though her first brush with violent death had changed her in some subtle way. He shifted uncomfortably in his saddle, trying to find a dry patch. "Has Miranda said anything more to you about Rodney?" he inquired casually.

"What's that, Hugo?" Felix asked, bringing his mount alongside his brother's. "Miranda and Rodney? No, nothing. In fact, I rather think she's been avoiding me of late. It's as I said before, Hugo, there's no understanding the fair sex at all. One minute they're as friendly as can be and before you know it they've turned a cold shoulder and are ignoring you."

"It must be difficult for her," Lord Romford said. "Don't forget that Miranda knew Justin held Rodney in high esteem. She is displaying a loyalty toward Rodney that can only be admired." Even as he spoke he wondered if this was the explanation he had been searching for.

"What! Determined to stand by an old friend and all that?" Felix commented. "If that's the case, I'd say she's a spunky little soul. Good for her."

They arrived back at Ramsden shortly after and were told by the footman that both ladies had retired for the day. Lord Romford experienced a moment's disappointment, for he had been looking forward to seeing Miranda.

"Miranda's probably still feeling the effects of her indisposition," Felix observed.

Lord Romford nodded and made to go upstairs. If he heard any sound from her room, he would check on her, he thought. However, the noise of the footman clearing his throat stopped him.

"M'lord," the footman said, "this note has just been delivered. The messenger said it was important." Lord Romford took it from the proffered tray and walked toward his study. Miranda would have to wait. Felix, unable to contain his curiosity, followed quickly.

"Who's it from?" he questioned. "Captain Jones?"

"No," Lord Romford answered, looking at the fine script. "My agent. He's in Tintern and wants to see me tonight."

"That's a nuisance," Felix said. "If only we had known, we could have stopped in this afternoon. Does the summons mean he has information on the paintings?"

Lord Romford nodded.

"But why the long face, Hugo?" Felix asked. "It means that we can solve the riddle."

"And if he has proof that Rodney is implicated, what do I do then?" Lord Romford's voice was heavy.

"Well, at least you'll know," Felix said practically.

"Just as I have reached the point of not wanting to know. Never mind, it's too late for that now." Lord Romford moved to his desk and opened a drawer as Felix watched in silence. He pulled out some papers until he exposed a small pistol. He looked at it for a few moments, and then, with some reluctance, took it out.

"I say, Hugo, do you really think that's necessary?" Felix exclaimed, knowing how much his brother hated firearms.

"I hope not," Lord Romford said tersely. "Let us say I think it's a wise precaution."

"Perhaps I should accompany you," Felix said, a genuine note of concern in his voice. "It would never do if something happened to you."

Lord Romford laughed at this and the tension that had been building up within him evaporated somewhat. "Your solicitude is heartening, Felix, but in this instance I think I'll do better alone. I have no intention of using this"—he paused as he pocketed the gun—"except in the most-dire circumstances. You will be of far greater use here, just in case Walter pays a surprise visit."

Felix looked dubious, as though he suspected he was being fobbed off. "I tell you, Hugo," he protested, "I don't like it. Walter wouldn't dare visit tonight. I mean, he'd have no excuse."

"But you'll do as I say, nonetheless, my boy," Lord Romford said. "I don't want the ladies left alone without a man in the house."

"That's ridiculous," Felix snorted. "The servants are here, and . . . and we can ask Jake to keep an eye open."

Lord Romford shook his head firmly. "No, Felix, my mind is made up, so let's have no more arguments. Now, I think I'll go and change and then have dinner."

Felix ground a fist into the palm of his hand moodily, but realizing that further argument would be useless, agreed to his brother's suggestion. "I'm beginning to understand how Miranda feels at being excluded when anything exciting happens," he said crossly.

"I hardly consider a tiresome ride into Tintern to meet my agent exciting," Lord Romford drawled sarcastically, although his eyes were alight with amusement. "Especially if the wretched man confirms our suspicions. I'll see you in the dining room in half an hour." He stopped at the door, chuckling as he looked his brother up and down. "And don't forget to give your boots to Watkins. Indeed, I would suggest you ask him to see what he can do with your jacket as well." He departed before Felix could recover himself sufficiently to say anything and went upstairs to dress for dinner. As he passed Miranda's door, he paused and raised a hand as though to knock, then changed his mind and continued on to his own quarters at the other end of the long corridor. He didn't want to disturb her if she was asleep.

Miranda had been moving about stealthily in her room when she heard footsteps. She froze where she stood, fearing that either her guardian or Felix would take it into their heads to check on her well-being if they heard any movement in her room. She was thankful she had done so when the footsteps came to a halt outside her door. She held her breath and only exhaled when she heard whoever it was move on. The last thing she wanted was anyone coming in and finding her fully dressed, holding the ring. Very quietly she resumed her activities of tapping the panels, one ear pressed to the wood, listening for a hollow sound. She had convinced herself that the coins lay somewhere behind the walls and was trying not to feel discouraged because two of the three paneled walls had yielded nothing.

It was still light outside, and placing the ring on her commode she picked up her book from it and took it to the sofa that stood in front of the windows. She sat down, curling her feet under herself and started to read. Shortly, though, her eyes grew heavy and soon she was fast asleep.

Both men were unusually quiet as they ate their dinner. Felix, still unhappy with his brother's plans of going into Tintern alone, had toyed with the idea of following him, but then decided against this in case he was detected. It would never do to incur the wrath of Hugo.

Lord Romford seemed oblivious to the conflicting emotions Felix was suffering, for he was too busy trying to come to terms with what he would have to do if his agent had bad news for him. Finally, when the last covers had been removed, he rose and excused himself.

"Don't drink too much brandy, Felix," he warned with a smile. "I don't want you falling asleep before I return."

Felix merely nodded his head and drew the decanter nearer. He splashed a small amount into his glass and raised it in salute to Lord Romford. However, as soon as Lord Romford had left the room, he added more of the amber liquid to his glass and drank of it deeply.

Dusk was falling as the groom led Lord Romford's horse out of the stables, and by the time Lord Romford had covered half the distance to Tintern, it was dark. Although he knew the way well, he was glad that the moon was out, casting a friendly light on the mud-caked road. He reached Tintern just after ten and as he didn't expect to be long, he merely tethered his horse to a hitching post in the cobblestoned courtyard of the inn. Following the instructions of Mr. Bryant, his agent, he went to a side entrance and knocked on the door. It was opened immediately and Mr. Bryant asked him in.

"Please excuse the informality," Mr. Bryant said, bowing deeply. "The landlord, a hearty sort of chap, as you must know, thought I'd like my own parlor room."

Lord Romford looked round and saw that he had, indeed, entered directly into a room.

"I had no idea that Phelps sported such a discreet meeting place," he murmured pleasantly, glancing down at Mr. Bryant. He was a small, bearded man, and Lord Romford towered above him.

Mr. Bryant laughed. "He convinced himself, I fear, that I was meeting a young lady and insisted I take this room so I could entertain my visitor without fear of interruption."

Lord Romford chuckled. "That sounds like Phelps. However, his curiosity will overcome his discretion and I daresay that in a few minutes he will find an excuse to come in."

"I hope he won't be too disappointed," Mr. Bryant countered jovially. "He can hardly gossip about your presence."

Lord Romford relaxed slightly. His agent's light banter indicated that the news he had was not too unpleasant. "What of my pictures?" he asked.

Mr. Bryant shook his head slightly and tugged at his beard. "The oddest thing," he remarked. "They have been bought by Viscount Brynmawr, and for a very tidy sum."

"Bought?" Lord Romford questioned, not bothering to conceal his surprise. "Are you certain?"

"Absolutely. And, in what has to be the strangest transaction ever."

"If Rodney bought them," Lord Romford said, more to himself than Mr. Bryant, "that would indicate he didn't steal them. But why would he do such a thing without consulting me?"

A troubled look crossed Mr. Bryant's face. "I think, my lord," he said tentatively, "that he was trying to protect his nephew."

"Walter!" Lord Romford exclaimed. "Of course. How obtuse of me. Sir Walter was the one selling them?"

Mr. Bryant nodded. "A month or two back. I haven't ascertained how Viscount Brynmawr found out, but he did and then ordered Mr. Purgavie, you might remember him, my lord, he bid on that Constable you bought, to buy your paintings on his behalf. He even instructed Mr. Purgavie not to negotiate a price, just to pay whatever was being asked."

Lord Romford, delighted by this news, shook Mr. Bryant's hand enthusiastically. "Thank you, Mr. Bryant," he said. "Thank you. You have done well."

Mr. Bryant coughed deprecatingly. "It was nothing, my lord," he said modestly. "Mr. Purgavie owed me a favor and once I had explained that the paintings had been stolen, he was happy to furnish me with the information. It was the only thing he could do to protect his reputation."

"Where are they now? The paintings, I mean."

"Unfortunately, Mr. Purgavie had already shipped them to Viscount Brynmawr at Rossfield before I questioned him, so I imagine that is where they are now."

"And Mr. Purgavie knows he is to make no mention of this to anyone, including the viscount?"

"I have his word, and he's as happy to let the matter be. As I said, he could be ruined if word leaked out that he had bought stolen artwork."

"That seems a trifle severe," Lord Romford remarked. "Especially since I hadn't notified anyone of the theft."

"But, my lord, " Mr. Bryant explained patiently, "he should have recognized those masterpieces as belonging to you, and his suspicions aroused when he knew I wasn't handling the sale."

"I see," Lord Romford said, suppressing a laugh with difficulty. The intrigues of art dealers always amused him. "But I suppose Viscount Brynmawr's instructions made him a little careless."

"Inexcusable, all the same."

"We have worked together for many years now, Mr. Bryant," Lord Romford observed.

"That's correct, my lord."

"What would you do if I ordered you to buy a painting that we both knew to be stolen?"

Mr. Bryant looked shocked at the very suggestion. "I hope you would never ask me to do such a thing, my lord," he said, "for I would have to sever our connection. I would never be party to such a thing."

Lord Romford nodded, satisfied with the reply. "Your ethics are highly commendable. Yet, in this particular instance I'm glad that Mr. Purgavie acted out of friendship for his client. He has saved us all from a great deal of embarrassment."

"You are certain, then, that Viscount Brynmawr will return the paintings?"

"He will more likely rehang them in my gallery without telling me in the hope that I will never discover they were ever missing."

Mr. Bryant shook his head dubiously. There was no accounting for the strange ways of the gentry and Lord Romford, realizing how odd his agent must think him, reassured him with a careless laugh. Now that the truth of the matter was out, he wanted to make as little fuss as possible. He knew he could trust Mr. Bryant not to repeat the story. Even so, it was as well to downplay it now. "I'm well satisfied with all you have told me," he said, "and I thank you again for all your help. It's gratifying to know that the mystery has been cleared up. Shall we appease Phelps's curiosity and go into the taproom for a drink? The need for secrecy has been lifted."

"That's most civil of you, my lord," Mr. Bryant said, obviously pleased by such an honor. "I'd like that very much."

Fourteen

When Miranda awoke it was dark. At first she thought the pins and needles she had in the leg curled beneath her had woken her, but as she tried to move it to the floor she became aware of a strange noise. Realizing, suddenly, that it was this that had caused her wakeful state, she gingerly inched her foot about and carefully straightened her leg. She wanted, desperately, to shake some life into it, but something held her back. Slowly, she looked around, and as her eyes became accustomed to the dark she could see that the handle of the large cupboard built into the recess near her was moving. She stiffened and had difficulty in suppressing a scream. Mentally scolding herself for being frightened, she sank back against the cushions and pretended she was still asleep. Through partially opened eyes she saw the flickering light of a candle as the cupboard door was pushed open and then a

man, masked and cloaked, stepped out onto the
floor. He looked about him, and although he gave
no indication that he had seen her, she couldn't be
certain that he hadn't. Terrified lest she make a
noise to betray her presence, she held her breath
and watched as the man went over to her bed.
Holding the candle down low, he grunted as he saw
the empty bed and then gave another grunt, one of
satisfaction, as he saw the ring. He picked it up and
peered at it closely for a few minutes before putting
it in his pocket. Then, very slowly, he turned his
gaze to the ceiling.

Miranda stared in fascination at the man. Any
fear she felt was coated by excitement, and as she
lay on the sofa she knew, instinctively, that the
intruder was Sir Walter. Such was his disguise,
though, she couldn't recognize him. Quietly exhal-
ing, she took another deep breath. Life was returning to her leg and it took all her self-control not to
move it. She didn't know how long she could hold
out, for the pain was now becoming quite intense.
Just as she was at the point of losing control, the
man turned and disappeared the way he entered,
making what seemed to Miranda an inordinate
amount of noise.

Quickly standing, Miranda hopped about on one
leg, shaking the other in a frenzied effort to get rid
of the pain. Very tentatively, she put it to the
ground, but it was useless. She couldn't walk. After
a few more minutes she could feel that the blood
was flowing more easily and without more ado she
hobbled after the man. She knew she should have
gone in search of her guardian or Felix, instead of
pursuing the stranger through the secret passageway, but she was afraid that if she wasted any more
time she would lose all trace of him. Also, she didn't

mind delaying the inevitable argument that was
bound to break out when she confessed to having
lost the ring.

Working in the dark it took her a while before she
could locate the mechanism to open the back panel
of the cupboard. She groped about until her fingers
encountered the small lever that she and Felix had
discovered several days earlier. She depressed this
and the panel slid back smoothly, revealing a flight
of stone steps. She peered into the blackness but
could neither see nor hear anything. Moving forward cautiously, one hand pressed against the
stone wall, the other lifting her skirts high above
her ankles, she slowly descended the steep steps,
pushing her daintily slippered foot to the edge of
the stonework before dropping it down.

"This is hopeless," she muttered crossly. "By the
time I have finished taking these stairs, the man
will be long gone."

She pushed her foot out one last time and
thankfully realized that she had reached the bottom. Still keeping one hand pressed against the
wall, she edged her way along the passage, but
unfortunately, in the darkness, she failed to see a
piece of rock protruding from the ground, and she
stumbled. She fell heavily on her knees, striking
the side of her head against the wall. She lay
motionless for a while as she caught her breath and
then began massaging her bruised joint. Refusing
to allow the agonizing pain to deter her, she stood
up and continued on down the passage. Finally,
after what seemed an eternity, she came to a blank
wall and finding the catch, opened this and stepped
out into the art gallery. There was enough light
from the moon for her to see that no one was about
and after brushing herself down she decided to

return to her bedroom to tidy herself up before going in search of her guardian. It was quite obvious that the man had already left the house.

She left the gallery and taking a lit candle from a holder in the wall, she limped upstairs. As she passed the large clock that stood in the hallway she glanced at the face and was surprised to see that it was well after midnight.

"That settles it," she told herself firmly, "I can't possibly wake Hugo up at such a late hour. It will just have to wait until the morning."

She reached her bedroom and walked in, her head bowed in thought. She was just about to light her lamp from the candle when she noticed that her pillow was on the floor and the gun exposed on the sheet beneath. She bent down to retrieve the pillow and as she straightened up she suddenly remembered how the intruder had stared up at the ceiling. She scrambled up on the bed and used the headboard to steady herself as she looked up. The dim light illuminated a large hole in the wall above the bed and by standing on the tips of her toes she managed to put her hand into it. Spreading her fingers, she felt around, but there was nothing there.

Puzzled, she sat down and absentmindedly lit the lamp and blew the candle out.

"Of course!" she exclaimed furiously, "that has to be the hiding place for the coins."

She got off the bed and dragged a straight-backed chair to the wall. Standing on this, she examined the frieze work and saw that the decorative pattern was of kings and queens. Only the face of one queen was missing. Clearly the face of the ring, when slotted in, opened the hiding hole.

"I have botched everything," she told herself

angrily. "Not only have I lost the ring, but the coins as well. And, what's more, I'm not sure who took them."

Her fury deepened as she realized how the intruder had hoodwinked her. He must have seen her on the sofa and had deliberately made a noise when he left the room, knowing that she would follow. The thought that she must have passed him in the passageway made her shudder, for undoubtedly he had doubled back, taken the coins and fled before she returned.

She stepped down from the chair and sat on it, wondering what to do next. She certainly was in no mood to face Lord Romford but with characteristic honesty, decided to make a clean breast of it immediately.

However, Lord Romford's empty chambers forced her to go downstairs again and after looking for him in his study and the library, she saw a light filtering through under the dining room door. She pushed it open and stared in surprise. There was no sign of Lord Romford, but Felix lay sprawled in his chair, fast asleep. The empty brandy decanter bore testament to his folly. She tried to shake him into wakefulness, but it was useless. He merely groaned, resettled himself and started to snore.

The whole scene was so ridiculous, Miranda laughed. "Felix, Felix," she chastised. "You silly boy. What use are you to anyone in this state? I'll just have to leave you and Hugo can deal with you, if he deigns to return."

She left the room quickly, thankful to be able to postpone the confrontation until morning. Lord Romford's absence from the house was perplexing, but she was too tired to give it much thought, and a few minutes later she was climbing into bed. She was asleep almost before her head touched the pillow.

The next morning, however, she regretted not having waited up for her guardian. It would have been better to have confessed everything then, than start the day with an argument. Indeed, as soon as she saw the expression on Lord Romford's face when she encountered him in the corridor, she knew she had made a grave mistake. His brows, pulled down close above his nose in a deep frown, indicated something had displeased him.

"Good morning, Hugo," she trilled softly, as she fell into step beside him. "Do . . . do you have a few minutes?"

"I do," he replied sharply, "if it's important."

"Ah! . . . Well . . . yes," she stammered, quite unnerved by his excessive ill-humor. "Perhaps it would be as well to wait until . . . until you have partaken breakfast."

"That won't make me any better tempered, Miranda," he said, "but don't worry, my black humor has, for once, been caused by someone other than you."

"Felix?" she countered in a small voice, remembering his drunken state. "You found him in the dining room?"

Lord Romford stopped and swung round to face her. "How did you happen to discover him?" he asked, his voice laced with sarcasm. "I thought you to be unwell and retired to your room yesterday."

"Actually, Hugo, if you must know, I was looking for you. However, had I known that his delicate condition would upset you so, I would have tried harder to rouse him." She tapped her foot on the carpet in frustration. Nothing ever went smoothly for her. She put a hand on Lord Romford's arm in an attempt to calm him. "Don't be too hard on him, Hugo," she pleaded. "It's the first time he's been in such a condition since he was sent down."

Not to be placated, Lord Romford shook her hand off. "I left him here with strict instructions to protect you ladies in the event that it became necessary, Miranda, so nothing anyone says will ease my temper. Felix was senseless when I returned last night. . . ."

". . . this morning," Miranda said before she could stop herself.

Lord Romford glared at her. "As you so rightly said, my dear, this morning . . . and of absolutely no use, had he been needed."

"Where were you, Hugo?" she asked in an effort to divert him.

"Let's not concern ourselves with that for the moment," he snapped. "What happened to cause you to go looking for me in the early hours?"

"Can . . . can we adjourn to your study?" she asked in one last attempt to be reasonable. "I think we would be more comfortable there."

Without a word, Lord Romford turned and continued on his way downstairs and Miranda, now totally exasperated, hurried after him.

Once their privacy was ensured, Miranda was uncertain as to how she should begin. She had never seen her guardian as angry as this.

"Well, Miranda," he prompted in a dangerously quiet voice, "what is it?"

Realizing there was nothing she could do to protect Felix, she plunged ahead. "A man came through the secret door in my room and took the coins which were hidden in the ceiling."

"Good God! Miranda," Lord Romford exclaimed, looking at her closely for signs of abuse. "Did he harm you? Are you all right? I swear, no matter what, Felix will pay for this."

"But Hugo," Miranda protested feebly, "there is nothing the matter with me except a bruised ego. Honestly, all he did was creep in, take the coins and leave. Even if both you and Felix had been near at hand, I swear you couldn't have helped me. It all happened so quickly."

With an effort, Lord Romford controlled himself. He eyed his ward suspiciously, as though not quite believing her. "Did you recognize him?" he asked finally.

"No . . . he was masked, but I think it was Sir Walter."

"What makes you so certain?"

"Well, I'm not. I only think it was he. Whoever it was found the ring on my commode and knew what to do with it. You see, the frieze work in my bedroom is patterned in miniatures of heads of kings and queens, only one queen face is missing. . . ."

". . . So the ring, placed in the hole, opens a secret hiding place?"

Miranda nodded, pleased that he was acting more reasonably.

"How did it come about that you were in possession of the ring?" he demanded.

Miranda colored. "I . . . er . . . I let something slip to Anita, which necessitated my telling her what had been going on."

"You what?" Lord Romford demanded in outrage. "Enough people are embroiled in this affair without adding another."

"It couldn't be helped, Hugo," Miranda interposed quickly. "And, as it turned out, Anita provided the answer to the riddle. It appears that

Queen Elizabeth spent the night once in my room and your ancestor called it the queen's boudoir."

"So you decided to play the heroine and took the ring to your room in the hope of finding the coins," Lord Romford finished for her scathingly. "Well, I hope you have learnt your lesson this time, and have come to realize the folly of your impetuous ways." He brushed aside the apology she tried to make and continued, "Last night I received some information that convinced me that Rodney was innocent . . . but now I'm not certain. I hope you are satisfied with the chaos you have created."

Miranda, near to tears at this unfair attack, turned away. "You . . . you don't have to be so beastly, Hugo," she said in a strangled voice. "I'm sorry." Even to her, the words sounded flat and she could sense she had further displeased her guardian with the trite comment. He hated warmed-over remarks and she had just made one.

"I have nothing more to say to you at the moment, Miranda. I'll see you later and we can discuss what to do next then."

In face of that dismissal, she had no alternative but to leave. He was right to be angry with her, but in this instance she had hoped he would show a little more tolerance. Maybe he would have done, had he not been in such a temper with Felix.

As neither Anita nor Felix was about, she took herself off to the stables. There was nothing she wanted more than to go for a good gallop across the fields. Jake quickly saddled a horse for her and after ensuring that Sarah and the puppies were well, she mounted and set off.

"Are you certain, my lady, that you don't want me to accompany you?" Jake asked in a fatherly fashion.

"No, thank you, Jake. If you see Felix, tell him the direction I took and that I'll meet him in the copse."

"Very good," Jake replied, shaking his head in disapproval. "I'll see that he catches up with you."

She spurred her horse and they trotted out of the courtyard. The sun felt warm on her back and after a while she reined in her mount and unbuttoned her jacket. Looking round to ensure no one was in sight, she untied the ribbons that held up her hair and it cascaded down her back. "That feels better," she said, shaking her heavy tresses. "Much better."

She had not been at the copse long, when she heard the sound of a horse approaching. She looked up and using one hand to shield her eyes from the bright light, looked across the field to see who it was. Recognizing Felix's horse, she sat down and waited for him. A few minutes later he arrived, flung himself off his horse and sat down beside her, groaning as he did so.

"You've no idea how my head aches," he complained. "And when Jake sent a message up to my room telling me that he had saddled my horse and wanted me to follow you, I wished you to the devil."

A look of annoyance swept across Miranda's face. "He takes too much on himself," she said. "How dare he disturb you?"

"I don't think he had a choice, old girl," Felix managed with a grimace. "Hugo ordered him to do it."

Miranda stood up abruptly and paced the grassy knoll. Here was yet another example of her guardian's imperious ways. Did he really think she was unable to take a solitary ride on his lands without getting into trouble? She looked down at Felix and saw his misery, so refrained from making any further comment on the subject. Instead, she knelt down and tried to comfort him. "You poor dear," she said. "I know how you must be feeling, for I saw you early this morning in a stupor."

Felix clutched his head dramatically. "Why did I do it?" he moaned. "Why?"

"I don't know," Miranda chuckled, "but you had better think up some excuse, for Hugo is absolutely livid. When I couldn't wake you, I left you in the chair. He found you when he came in and I presume took you up to your bed."

Felix looked at her blankly. "I don't remember a thing," he said. "Why is he so cross?"

"I think because you were supposed to protect us and got drunk instead. . . . "

"I know that," Felix said crossly.

". . . And we had an intruder."

"Oh! No! Who? What was it all about? No wonder he's in such high dudgeon."

Briefly, Miranda told him of the events that had taken place last night, and by the time she had finished Felix was in a most despondent state.

"Egads!" he uttered miserably. "I don't look forward to my interview with Hugo. I don't suppose he mentioned the outcome of his meeting last night?"

"Honestly, Felix, he was so angry he could hardly speak. Especially when I told him that I had confided everything in Anita."

"Why on earth did you do that?" Felix asked in surprise.

"I . . . I had my reasons," Miranda responded evasively. She certainly didn't want to confide in Felix. "But about last night, Hugo did say something about receiving information that made him believe Rodney was innocent, though after hearing my story I think he changed his mind. Where *did* he go last night?"

"To meet with his agent, who presumably had news of the paintings. I overimbibed because I was furious he wouldn't take me."

His sad expression reminded Miranda so much of a naughty puppy she couldn't help but smile. "Poor Felix," she commiserated. "I know how you feel. Your brother has the most annoying ability of making us both feel superfluous."

A determined look settled on his face and he stood up. "There's no need for us to sit her moping. Why don't we ride over to Rossfield and find out what's going on?"

Without another word, Miranda went over and caught her horse. Leading him over to a convenient log, she mounted and set off toward Rossfield, looking over her shoulder to see that Felix followed.

"Sometimes, Felix," she said as he drew alongside, "you have good ideas. Even if we don't gather any answers, we at least can show Hugo he cannot intimidate us."

Fifteen

After dismissing Miranda, Lord Romford sat at his desk for a long while. He thought about dropping a note to the viscount, asking him to call, but then decided to go to Rossfield himself. Last night, as soon as he had returned home, he had gone directly to the art gallery and had been highly gratified to see that the original paintings had been restored. His good humor had lasted until he found Felix, and then, for some inexplicable reason, he felt an anger he had never experienced before. He thought his fury was caused by his brother's disregard for his wishes, but even that didn't really account for his bitter reaction. Now, after listening to Miranda's story, he began to understand himself. His real concern had been his fear that something would happen to the chit. And, if he were really honest, he should have directed his anger toward himself, not Felix, for not asking his agent to Ramsden.

He went out to the stables and on discovering from Jake that Miranda had ridden off unescorted he ordered word be sent to rouse Felix with instructions for him to go after her. He knew that if he rode after her, she would resent his presence, but until he found out what was really going on at Rossfield, he didn't want her out alone.

He rode over to the viscount's at a leisurely pace, going over in his mind exactly what he wanted to say. He would make mention of the paintings and that, naturally, would lead him to talk of last night's intruder. For, if indeed Rodney had returned them last night, he and not Sir Walter could have been the person Miranda saw. And it was that fact that disturbed him now. Whatever, he knew it was going to be a difficult interview, but the time for plain speaking had arrived and he was determined to clear the air once and for all.

Taking the short cut through the bottom woods, he approached Rossfield from the south. Knowing the viscount's stables to be in poor condition, he decided to leave his horse in the front driveway. As he rounded the last bend, the house came into full view. His experienced eye picked out the decaying stonework that Miranda had failed to notice. Several slates were missing from the roof.

"A good thing Rodney doesn't have servants that live in," he said disapprovingly, "else they'd get soaked every time it rained."

Lord Romford was proud of the immaculate living conditions he maintained for his servants, considering it a small recompense for the hard life they endured. Consequently he experienced no great turnover in staff and enjoyed an unusual loyalty that was the envy of many of his friends. His servants never gossiped, except amongst themselves, and Watkins had, on at least two occasions he knew of, come to fisticuffs with Lord Denbigh's valet when that unfortunate individual had made some scathing remark about Lord Romford's dress.

He reined in his horse and slid out of the saddle. "I won't be long, Firefly," he reassured the gentle creature, and walked up to the front door. He rang the bell and waited. After several minutes had elapsed he banged the heavy brass door knocker, the noise echoing throughout the house. Still no one came. Impatiently, he pushed the oak door, and with a creak, it opened. He looked inside and frowned. The front hall was deserted. Indeed, the whole house seemed empty.

"Is anyone at home?" he shouted as he stepped inside.

A sound from upstairs broke the silence and he looked toward the head of the stair expectantly.

"Just a moment," someone answered. "I'll be down directly."

Lord Romford frowned, not liking the situation. Where were the servants? he wondered. And whose voice had responded? Seized with impatience, he started for the stairs when Sir Walter appeared, tying the belt of his gold brocade robe. He looked quite ill in the morning light that filtered through the grimy windows.

"Is something amiss?" Lord Romford asked. "Where's Rodney?"

Sir Walter, in a dramatic gesture, put a hand to his forehead. "If I knew the answer to that, Hugo," he drawled, "I wouldn't be here. I fear he has left for France, but . . . "

"France?" Lord Romford interrupted in disbelief. "Have you taken leave of your senses?"

Sir Walter gave a weary laugh and dropped his hand to his pocket. "I wish I had, but I'm afraid that my dear uncle has been found out and, rather than stay and face his accusers, decided to flee."

"You talk in riddles," Lord Romford said in exasperation. It was always the same when he had to talk to Sir Walter. "Can we not go to the study and talk rationally?"

"By all means, Hugo, please be my guest. I'm afraid I cannot offer you any refreshment, though, for Rodney dismissed all the servants yesterday."

Lord Romford raised his eyebrows in surprise. "You mean he knew he would be gone today?" He didn't bother to conceal the skepticism he felt at his own suggestion, for what Sir Walter was implying deserved to be treated with contempt. All the hostility he had felt for Sir Walter over the years that he had known him came to the fore now. He eyed him haughtily.

Seemingly unperturbed by Lord Romford's rudeness, Sir Walter sauntered down the stairs, an unpleasant smile playing on his thin lips. "I'm not suggesting anything," he said softly. "However, I think after you have heard what I have to say, you will not be surprised by his absence."

His flippant manner irked Lord Romford, but he followed him into the study without comment, making a determined effort to control his temper. It was something he'd never had much trouble in controlling before had become Miranda's guardian, but prior to that his well-ordered life had given him little to be cross about. Now, he realized, he had been excessively out of sorts, especially with Miranda. Not that she didn't deserve it most of the time.

A laugh from Sir Walter cut into his thoughts and he turned his attention back to the matter on hand.

"An unnecessary precaution this," Sir Walter was saying as he closed the door. "There is absolutely no one here to listen to our conversation."

Lord Romford ignored this, anxious now to hear what Sir Walter had to say. "What is the truth, Walter?" he asked brusquely. "Has Rodney really left for France?"

"It may come as something of a shock to you, Hugo," Sir Walter began, "but I'm sure that Rodney is in the Frenchies' pay. . . . " He paused, waiting for some reaction. But Lord Romford merely waved a hand for him to continue. "I . . . I stumbled across something recently that made me suspect him and was on the verge of getting the necessary proof when my informant was killed."

"Anthony Roberts," Lord Romford said.

Sir Walter nodded. "It seems that Rodney was trying to raise money for his friends' and used this man Roberts to search for those coins of yours."

Again Lord Romford maintained his silence. He was tempted to inquire about the paintings, but something in Sir Walter's manner held him back.

"Anyway," Sir Walter continued, "on my last visit to Rossfield a few weeks ago, I discovered Roberts lurking about the stables. I asked him what he was up to and . . . and after a bit of persuasion he confessed everything to me."

"What method did you employ to induce him to talk?" Lord Romford asked, his curiosity momentarily roused. Sir Walter had always appeared to be too much of a dandy to resort to fisticuffs.

"I . . . I, well, I tightened his necktie until he had difficulty in breathing and then threatened to take him to the local magistrate." Sir Walter's expression was one of distaste as he spoke, as though he regretted this violent act. "I don't, as a rule, approve of such tactics, but I was desperate."

"Quite so," Lord Romford sympathized. "Most unpleasant, but one presumes your strategy was successful?" Had any of Lord Romford's friends been present, they would have recognized the thinly veiled contempt in his voice, but Sir Walter, apparently satisfied that his story sounded plausible, pressed on.

"He, Roberts, that is, said that he had found the ring and had arranged to meet Rodney in order to give it to him. Frankly, Hugo, I was shocked. I found it difficult to believe that my uncle would actually do such a thing."

"You let Roberts go?"

Sir Walter nodded. "I didn't know what else to do. Family honor and all that dictated my action."

Lord Romford sat down, his expression thoughtful. The story sounded reasonable enough, except for the omission of the paintings. For if the viscount was really trying to raise money, why would he have bought them from Purgavie and restored them to Ramsden? He looked at Sir Walter, hoping to see some outward sign that he was lying, but Sir Walter was staring out of the window, a bland expression on his face. "Did you ask Rodney if any of this were true?"

"I . . . I was considering that, when I heard that Roberts had been shot and had died as a result of the wound the day after I had spoken with him."

"And you assumed Rodney was responsible?" Lord Romford suggested helpfully.

"It did cross my mind and I decided that until I could actually prove anything, my most prudent course was to keep silent. And I did, until last night. I came home late and surprised Rodney in here looking at the coins. We had a fearful argument and . . . and that's all I remember until you arrived just now. We drank some brandy and I think Rodney must have drugged mine."

"You are saying, then, that the servants were dismissed yesterday?"

"Yes, it's as I said earlier. And, what is more, Rodney said that he had dismissed them because he didn't want anyone to find out what he was up to."

"You were fortunate Rodney saw fit to spare you, then," Lord Romford murmured.

Sir Walter shook his head. "He knew he could rely on me to keep quiet about it."

"Of course," Lord Romford said, attempting to disguise how perturbed he was, "the family honor and all that."

Sir Walter agreed mournfully. "He knows I won't say anything."

"But, dammit, Walter, if this is really the truth, we simply can't let him get away. Where has he gone?"

"If I knew, I wouldn't say. This is something that concerns my family, Hugo, and you must leave that decision to me. There will be an uproar if the truth were to leak out. I shall, with your help of course, spread the word that for reasons of health and a broken heart, Rodney has gone to Europe."

"And if he returns?"

"He won't. I told him I would expose him if he did."

"I see," Lord Romford said quietly. "Obviously, I must respect your wishes. Did he, perchance, say anything about some paintings?" He posed the question casually but looked at Sir Walter carefully and was certain that he paled before shaking his head in denial.

"No . . . no, nothing at all. Are you missing any?"

"No," Lord Romford replied truthfully. "I was just wondering, for I know he was evaluating a few for some friends of mine in London. It would have been very easy for him to have taken them with him. But, then again, it might have seemed an unnecessary risk."

"That's the answer, certainly," Sir Walter agreed quickly. "He seemed delighted by the value of the coins. I think he was satisfied that he would be able to raise enough money by selling them to live comfortably."

An uneasy silence fell between the two men and after a while Lord Romford rose. He knew he should extend his hand, but it was a gesture he couldn't bring himself to make. The viscount might very well be guilty, but that didn't make him feel friendly toward Sir Walter. "If there is anything I can do, please let me know," he said after a pause. "I'll be at Ramsden for at least another week."

Sir Walter bowed foppishly and Lord Romford looked at him in disgust. He got the distinct impression that the man was gloating over something. He took his leave and let himself out.

Once outside, he took a couple of deep breaths to clear his head. There were still many questions left unanswered, but basically Sir Walter's story made sense. With an impatient shrug of his shoulders, Lord Romford whistled for his horse and waited for Firefly to respond. A feeling of sadness washed over him. That a man he had considered a friend was capable of such duplicity was a difficult pill to swallow. He didn't want to believe what he had heard, but Sir Walter had been very convincing. And what was he to tell Miranda? The truth? He knew the answer to be yes, yet he was reluctant to hurt her again.

"Dammit, dammit!" he muttered in frustration. "I always seem to be the bearer of bad news." The gentle pressure of his horse's nose nuzzling at his pocket for sugar forced his thoughts back to the present. Digging his hand into his pocket he palmed a lump of sugar and fed it to Firefly. As he did so, he saw two riders approaching and with eyes narrowed he watched them draw near. For a fleeting second he was hopeful that one of them would be the viscount, but then experienced a severe letdown when he recognized his brother and Miranda. Momentarily forgetting that he had last parted from Miranda on bad terms, he waved them over.

"You wanted us, Hugo?" Miranda asked belligerently.

Lord Romford stared at her bleakly, surprised by her tone, and then, recalling his earlier abrupt dismissal of her, frowned. She was going to be difficult to handle in her present mood. "Yes," he said. "I have some distressing news and would like to see you both, along with Anita, in my study."

Miranda shot Felix a defiant look, but Felix turned away. He could tell by the set of his brother's shoulders that Lord Romford was upset and realized that it had nothing to do with his own reprehensible behavior.

"Can it not wait?" Miranda asked peevishly. "I want to see Rodney."

"We can return later," Felix interposed hurriedly. "Come, I'll race you back." He turned his horse and trotted off.

Miranda, obviously undecided about what to do, looked toward Rossfield and then at Felix. Lord Romford mounted Firefly and drew alongside Miranda. "If you wish to return after you have heard my news, I won't stand in your way," he said quietly.

The flat despair in his voice made Miranda look at him closely, and after a moment she nodded and started after Felix. She had never seen her guardian look so worried.

Anita greeted them upon their return, demanding to know where they all had been. "I declare I have been worried to death, and Mrs. Branley has been of no help."

"What! Has she finally recovered?" Felix asked in an attempt to be light-hearted. "Do you want her to hear what you have to say, Hugo?"

"No," Lord Romford said brusquely. "Let us proceed to my study as quickly and quietly as possible. We can reassure her later that we are still in one piece."

Anita, puzzled by her cousin's curtness, fell into step beside Miranda. "Has something befallen Rodney?" she whispered anxiously.

Miranda shrugged her shoulders. "We'll find out soon enough," she answered. "We met Hugo at Rossfield and he ordered us to come back here."

As soon as they reached the study, Lord Romford gestured for them to be seated while he closed the door. In somber tones he told them all that he had learned from Sir Walter.

"Good heavens!" Felix exclaimed. "Who ever would have believed such a thing of Rodney?"

"I don't," Anita and Miranda said in unison. "Sir

Walter has to be lying," Miranda continued as she held Anita's arm consolingly. "Rodney is far too honorable to be mixed up in such perfidy."

The pinched look about her mouth was evidence of the shock she felt at the news of the viscount's treachery and as Lord Romford looked at her he experienced an overwhelming desire to hold her close and comfort her. "I'm sorry, Miranda," he said at length, "but until Rodney comes forward to refute Walter's accusations there is nothing we can do."

"But the coins," Miranda protested, "they're yours. Surely that's reason enough to search for him."

Lord Romford shook his head. "No. I have given Walter my word not to look for Rodney." He left the room. He had to get away from Miranda, for the bleak look that had descended on her face at his news had completely unmanned him. Felix, worried about his brother's state, hurried after him.

Miranda stared after the men thoughtfully until Anita's sobbing penetrated her musing. Quickly, she put her arm about Anita and tried to comfort her.

"Oh! Miranda, I know something terrible has happened. I know it. What can I do? What can I do?"

"There, there, my dearest Anita. I have a plan. Trust me, please. Go to your room now, for it would never do for Hugo or Felix to see you in this state, and when I return I'm sure I'll have better news for you." She stood up, pulling Anita with her.

"I . . . I can't think why Hugo would believe such nonsense," Anita cried. "He is so sensible, normally. . ."

"I know . . . I know," Miranda soothed, pushing

Anita toward the door. "I'll be as quick as I can, so please don't worry." She finally persuaded Anita to go upstairs and rest, with the promise that she would drop by the sitting room to see Mrs. Branley before she went out. However, such was her haste to be gone that she completely forgot to do so, and only remembered when she had arrived at Rossfield.

Sixteen

The plan Miranda had mentioned to Anita was actually no more than an ill-formed idea, and in her usual impetuous way, she arrived at Rossfield without actually knowing what she would say to Sir Walter. Somewhat naively, she felt that if she confronted him with the information that she had recognized him as the intruder last night, he would be forced to tell her the truth. It didn't occur to her that by doing so she was placing herself in further danger.

However, when she arrived, she found the house to be deserted. After a fruitless search of all the downstairs rooms she gave up. Sir Walter was definitely not about. On a sudden impulse, she went to the stables and discovered that the viscount's favorite hunter was missing, but was able to reassure herself that Sir Walter must have taken it to keep up the pretense of his theory that Rodney was the guilty one.

"He must have done," she reasoned, "and I do believe I know how I can find out where he's gone." She picked her way out of the rubble that strewed the stable floor and set off for Ramsden, her mind in a positive spin as she tried to think of how she could slip out of the house without anyone's knowledge, dressed in Felix's clothes. "I'll show you what loyalty to a friend means, Hugo," she muttered. "I'll prove that Rodney is innocent."

Lord Romford's quick acceptance of Sir Walter's story had been a severe disappointment. She had thought him to be more astute, even though there were mitigating circumstances. Maybe she should excuse his lapse, for it was obvious that he lacked the intuition of a woman.

"That's it," she told herself, relieved to have found a reason for his lack of faith. "And, I shall tell Anita that that is the case."

Upon her return to Ramsden she found Felix and Anita seated in the library. As soon as Felix saw her, he put his fingers to his lips.

"Sssh!" he whispered. "We're hiding from Mrs. Branley."

Miranda tiptoed in and closed the door quietly behind her. "Why are we whispering?" she asked softly. "These walls are so thick, nothing would penetrate them."

"Not the walls, you goose, but the sound of our voices carries through the chimney flues."

Anita, who seemed to have recovered her spirits somewhat, smiled wanly. "She was most upset that we ignored her this morning and . . . and you forgot to see her. . . . "

" . . . I know," Miranda interrupted contritely. "I

only remembered when I reached Rossfield. But I'll go in and see if I can't appease her."

"It's too late for that," Felix said with a laugh. "She's retired to bed in umbrage."

"For another three weeks?" Miranda asked hopefully.

Anita shook her head. "No, just for a rest. She will be down shortly. What . . . what of your trip, Miranda? Did you discover anything?"

"Sir Walter has vanished, at least I couldn't find him."

"But . . . but Rodney? What of him?" Anita's voice shook, her composure lost.

Miranda gave her a sympathetic look, knowing it to be useless to hide the truth from her. "I'm afraid I don't know, Anita. I think I should tell Hugo that the house seems deserted and let him decide what we should do next."

"He's out," Felix informed her. "I think this business, especially Rodney's involvement, has shaken him badly and he wants time to be by himself."

Miranda was pleased to hear this. It was gratifying to know that he could be human and experience a depression of the spirits.

Anita, unable to sit quietly a moment longer, suddenly stood up. "If . . . if no one objects," she said with some determination, "I'd like to go back to Rossfield. You may think it sounds peculiar, Felix, but I think something awful has happened to Rodney and I would like to search his house thoroughly."

Felix, who until that moment had not considered Anita's reactions odd, stood up and gallantly offered to escort her. "Do you return with us, Miranda?"

"No . . . no," Miranda said hesitantly. "I don't think I have the energy." She had difficulty hiding the delight she felt, and feigned a yawn. With everyone out of the way she would have no difficulty slipping out of the house. "I think I will rest for a while, before the next round of excitement."

Anita was too concerned over the fate of her beloved to notice the note of mischief in Miranda's voice. "I'll just fetch my shawl, Felix, and we can be on our way." As she hurried out of the library, she turned and said to Miranda, "For goodness' sake, don't forget to see Mrs. Branley when she comes down."

By the time Anita and Felix arrived at Rossfield, Anita had worked herself into a great state of agitation. She did her best to conceal this from Felix. However, she needn't have worried, for Felix was deep in thought and wasn't paying too much attention to her strange behavior. Miranda was up to something, he was convinced of it, but the trouble was finding out what. Deciding that he would question her when he returned, he turned his attention to his cousin.

"I say, Anita, who exactly have we come here in search of?"

"Rodney, of course," Anita said. "Miranda and I are certain that Sir Walter is behind his disappearance. He . . . he . . . that is, Rodney, would be incapable of doing all those things Sir Walter accused him of."

"I'm inclined to agree," Felix said, "although, if he is innocent, he has certainly acted strangely and, I must add, secretively."

Anita refrained from answering. She couldn't deny Felix's allegations. The door to Rossfield was open, and Felix put a cautionary arm on Anita's.

"Best let me precede you," he said gruffly, and walked on ahead. He scanned the front hall but saw nothing ominous and so beckoned Anita in. "Miranda must have left it like that," he said. "Come, let us begin our search. I'll go upstairs and you take the ground floor."

The noise of an upstairs door creaking caused Felix to break off and both of them looked toward the sound with some trepidation. They could see the shadow of a man looming large on the landing wall and Felix quickly stood in front of Anita.

"Hullo!" he called out sternly. "Who's there?"

"Aha! Felix," Lord Romford said, stepping out of the shadows, "and Anita, I beg your pardon, I didn't see you at first."

"What are you doing here, Hugo?" Felix demanded. "You gave us quite a fright."

Lord Romford smiled briefly. "I see I must beg your pardon again. I would have announced my presence earlier had I known to expect you." He looked around the main hall. "Where's Miranda? Did she not come with you?"

"No," Anita replied. "She was here earlier and discovered that Sir Walter had vanished. We decided to come and see what was happening for ourselves."

"What decided you to return, Hugo?" Felix asked.

"I don't really know," Lord Romford said as he descended the stairs. "Something about Walter's story bothered me, but it seems as though I am too late to ask any more questions."

"What do you mean?" Anita demanded nervously. "Is he dead?"

"Good heavens, no!" Lord Romford said hastily. "I should have said that he had departed. I was just upstairs checking on his clothes. All gone. As are Rodney's."

"Oh!" Anita responded flatly, unable to think of a more suitable reply. She had convinced herself that the viscount was still somewhere in the house, but this piece of news seemed to preclude that. "Are you absolutely certain, Hugo?"

"Miranda and Anita have formed this idea that Walter has done something unspeakable to Rodney," Felix interceded as he saw the puzzled expression on his brother's face. "That's really why we're here, to see if we can't find any bodies."

"Really, Felix," Anita said with some agitation, "please don't even jest about such a thing."

"Well, there are no signs of anything untoward," Lord Romford reassured Anita. "Not upstairs, anyway."

"What about down here, and in the cellars?" Anita persisted, the alarm she felt over her beloved's fate giving her courage to speak so. "Are you truly certain no one is here?"

Lord Romford, becoming increasing astonished by Anita's insistent manner, shook his head. "I haven't looked in the cellars yet," he said slowly. "I can only suggest that we all go down and take a look." He moved toward the nether regions. "If my memory serves me correctly, the entrance to the cellars is by the pantry."

Anita followed him quickly. "Does it not seem strange to you, Hugo, that no one is about? Surely, Rodney wouldn't leave his house completely unattended."

"I wouldn't have thought so, unless he had no intention of returning to England. Then he wouldn't worry about the upkeep of Rossfield."

"I know he w—" Anita began but was interrupted by Felix.

"Hugo, Hugo," Felix was saying. "Did you notice this?" He indicated the servants' dining hall, a small room off the passage leading to the kitchens. "It looks as though a bit of a struggle took place in here." He walked in and waited for the other two to join him.

Two dining chairs had been overturned. The white linen tablecloth was half off the table, looking as though it had been dragged by someone, leaving the water glasses and silverware in disarray.

Anita gave a startled exclamation as she saw the mess. "I know something simply dreadful has befallen Rodney. I know it!"

Lord Romford, who was standing right behind her, looked at Felix with raised brows. The intensity with which Anita spoke betrayed her feelings. "It would certainly seem as though Rodney's servants have suffered a strange fate," he said, pointedly stressing "servants." "Shall we go to the cellars and see if they are there?"

Anita blushed, realizing that she had betrayed herself. "Of . . . of course. It would seem the obvious place to look," she muttered in embarrassment.

The cellar doors were locked and bolted and as Lord Romford tried to prise them open he asked Felix to pass a candle.

"The door seems to be well secured," Felix observed. "One would think that Rodney housed a remarkable collection of wine."

Lord Romford grunted as he drew the last bolt. "My instinct tells me that wine is not the only thing stored down there. Here, give me the candle and you stay at the top with Anita." He took the light and started down, peering into the dark. He felt something brush against his leg and kicked it away, thinking it a rat. However, he realized his mistake when he heard Anita's voice calling a cat to her side. The glimmer from his light cast long shadows and soon he was able to discern the shapes of the wine racks. A muffled noise caught his attention and he moved toward it quickly. Staring into the semi-darkness he finally saw the shapes of three men, bound and gagged. Calling to Felix to come down and help, he dropped to his knee and fixed the candle on a flagstone.

"I'll have you free in a trice," he said grimly, untying the gag of the only servant he recognized, Wilkins, the viscount's valet. He felt, rather than saw, Felix join him and soon they had all the men free. "Just move about as much as you can to restore your circulation," he advised. "We can talk of this when we get upstairs."

"Very good, m'lord," Wilkins mumbled, rubbing his wrists and arms. "Though I wouldna' mind getting out of 'ere soonest, as this cellar is right rat-infested."

Felix looked about him distastefully but, unable to see anything move, merely shrugged his shoulders and proffered an arm to Humphries, the elderly footman. "I'll help you up the stairs," he said. "Take them carefully."

Anita fussed over the servant and directed Felix to return. "Please look around some more, maybe Rodney is down there somewhere."

"No one but me, Mr. Wilkins and Fred were down there," the footman advised, a tremble in his voice. "It's a terrible time we've 'ad. Spent the whole night down there we did and couldn't even talk amongst ourselves because of the gags."

"That's appalling," Anita exclaimed. "Who on earth was responsible?"

The footman shook his head. "I dunno as I can answer that, miss. See we was 'aving our supper when this masked man came in and ordered us to stand up and then I think I were 'it on the 'ead, for I don't remember too much after that."

Anita took him by the arm and led him to the servants' hall, clucking sympathetically. "I'm so sorry," she said with as much patience as she could muster, although her concern for the viscount made it difficult for her to remain calm. "Do you have any idea who the man was?"

"No," the footman replied forlornly. "None at all. We'll 'ave to wait and see if Mr. Wilkins can 'azard a guess."

"Mr. Wilkins?" Anita queried distractedly.

"'Is lordship's valet."

Anita sat down. She felt sick with apprehension and the lines of worry stood out on her ashen face. Lord Romford's voice caused her to start and she turned away as she tried to compose herself. It was becoming painfully obvious to her that something awful had, indeed, befallen the viscount.

"I'll not keep you long," Lord Romford was saying. "I'd like to ascertain what exactly happened and then we can proceed from there. Mr. Wilkins, do you have any idea?"

"I wish I could 'elp, m'lord. The fact of the matter is we was caught unawares by a man whose face was hidden behind a mask." His chest seemed to puff out with importance as he spoke. "And, afore we could do owt, begging your pardon, m'lord, anything, Humphries was 'it on the 'ead and we was told the same thing would 'appen to us if we didn't obey."

"But would you state categorically that the man was not Viscount Brynmawr?" Lord Romford asked.

Anita held her breath, knowing that she would scream if Mr. Wilkins answered in the affirmative. But she relaxed slightly as she saw him shake his head.

"No, m'lord," was his dignified response, "it was not. I caught sight of the shoes the man was wearing and I know that 'is lordship don't own a pair as vulgar as that. Also, it was quite obvious that the man disguised 'is voice, for 'e spoke sort of 'igh, effeminate you might say, which again is something 'is lordship wouldn't be capable of doing, 'im being of such a deep voice."

Lord Romford nodded, satisfied with the answer. He didn't want to press the issue, but he had made up his mind that the man had been Sir Walter. "When did you last see Viscount Brynmawr?"

Mr. Wilkins scratched his head. "It were just after dinner 'ad been served. 'Is lordship sent for me and asked me to dismiss all the servants, give them a few days' holiday 'e said, all excepting me, Fred and 'Umphries."

"You have been with him a long time, have you not?" Lord Romford asked. Wilkins nodded. "Did he often stay in residence with just three servants?"

"I did think it a bit odd," Wilkins concurred, "but"—he shrugged his shoulders—"it were not really my place to question 'is orders."

"I see," Lord Romford said thoughtfully, wishing he knew the reason behind the viscount's strange command. The viscount's actions to this point were odd: odd, that is, if he were innocent. "And his clothes? Did you pack those for him?"

"Clothes, m'lord," Wilkins asked, totally mystified. "They was all 'anging in 'is closet last time I looked."

"Very good," Lord Romford said briskly. "And Sir Walter, when did you last see him?"

Mr. Wilkins looked to Humphries to answer and Humphries shuffled uncomfortably, obviously not liking to be the center of attention in such august company. Anita, understanding his predicament, hastened to set him at ease.

"What time was it that he went out?" she prompted.

"Ah! Well, let me see. That would 'ave been late afternoon. I don't know exactly the hour because the clock in the 'all don't work."

"Thank you, Humphries," Lord Romford said. "I can see there is nothing to be gained by questioning you further. Would any of you object to staying here a few more days until we have cleared this matter up?" He looked at the three men commandingly and smiled encouragingly at Mr. Wilkins.

"I can only speak for myself, m'lord, but I wouldn't dream of leaving until I gets my orders from 'is lordship. It wouldn't be proper."

"Of course not," Lord Romford agreed. "And you, Humphries? And Fred?" Both men nodded their assent and Lord Romford thanked them for their cooperation. "I know I can rely on your discretion over this unfortunate episode, at least until we have discovered Viscount Brynmawr's whereabouts. If you hear from him in the meantime, I would be grateful if you could send word to Ramsden."

The servants were, quite obviously, relieved that someone had taken control of the situation and Mr. Wilkins expressed his appreciation for Lord Romford's forbearance. "I know 'is lordship respects you, m'lord, and I'm sure he'd wish us to do as you ask until he returns."

Lord Romford smiled. "I don't think it will be long before we hear something. Felix, Anita, if you're ready, shall we go?"

Anita rose reluctantly. She couldn't shake the feeling that the viscount was somewhere in the house. She was about to express her thoughts when she saw Lord Romford frown and shake his head slightly. "Yes, Hugo," she replied meekly after a moment's hesitation, and left the room.

Seventeen

The three returned to Ramsden quickly. Anita, quite overcome by her indiscreet behavior, resolved firmly not to say anything unless someone spoke to her first. She also resolved to return to Rossfield, by herself, later, and see if she couldn't find a trace of the viscount. Her belief in his innocence remained unshaken.

However, on their arrival home, all thoughts of the viscount were pushed from her mind when she discovered Mrs. Branley pacing the sitting room in a great state of agitation.

Lord Romford was the first at her side and it took all his powers of persuasion to calm the elderly lady sufficiently to enable them to understand her outrage.

"It's too much for anyone to bear," she gasped, dabbing at her eyes with her silk handkerchief. "I cannot think you to be so inhumane as to force me to stay a moment longer, Hugo. If you do, then be prepared to accept the consequences."

Lord Romford looked to Anita for help. "What is it, Clarissa?" she asked calmly. "Has Miranda upset you?"

"Don't mention that name in my presence," Mrs. Branley groaned, clutching her heart dramatically. "When I think of all the time I have wasted trying to groom her. . . ."

"What has she done this time, Clarissa?" Lord Romford interrupted, a grim look settling on his face.

"Up to! Up to! She's always up to something and it's usually no good. Well, this time she's gone too far, even for me. . . ."

"You mustn't get so worked up, Clarissa," Anita soothed. "If you could just tell us what happened, then we will know what to do."

"It's too late to do anything, for she left more than an hour ago. . . ."

"Did she say where she was going?" Anita pressed.

"No . . . no," Mrs. Branley snapped, "but there she was, bold as a brass farthing, dressed in your clothes, Felix, looking every inch the boy she's always wanted to be. Calmly, yes, calmly, telling me that she would be back in time for dinner." She shuddered as she spoke, leaving her audience in no doubt of her utter disapproval.

Lord Romford let out an exasperated sigh. "Cast your mind back, Clarissa. Are you certain Miranda made no mention of where she was going, dressed as she was?"

"Well . . . " Mrs. Branley conceded, fanning herself limply, "it sounded garbled to me, but mayhap you can fathom it. She took your horse,

Hugo, for speed, and said that she had to follow someone to Newport." She broke off to gaze mournfully at Lord Romford. "Mark my words, it'll be around the whole shire in a trice if anyone recognizes her. And that, surely, will give the viscount an excuse to end the engagement."

Before she had finished speaking, Lord Romford moved to the bellrope and tugged it angrily.

"Now, if you will excuse me," Mrs. Branley continued, "I think I will retire. The events of the day have so exhausted me, I do not think I can keep my eyes open another second."

"That is probably the best idea you have had today, Clarissa," Lord Romford said tersely. "If you are still of a mind to leave, I'll instruct Jake to ready the carriage for your journey tomorrow."

"If I'm sufficiently recovered," she responded weakly. "I'll . . . I'll let you know in the morning."

"But you said you wanted to go . . . " Lord Romford began but, seeing the tears trickling down her cheeks, rolled his eyes upward. "Then you must stay for as long as you want," he continued impatiently. "Just let me know when you feel up to the journey." He broke off as the door opened. "Ah! Watkins," he greeted the butler in relief. "I need my phaeton readied immediately." The butler bowed and allowed Mrs. Branley to exit before he withdrew.

Felix, who hadn't spoken since leaving Rossfield, turned to his brother, his face aglow with excitement. "I knew the brat was up to something. She was far too quiet when we left her. In fact, I had made up my mind to force her to tell me what she had planned."

"It's a pity both of you didn't stay here with her, instead of traipsing all over the countryside looking for Rodney," Lord Romford said scathingly, his temper once more on the rise because of his ward's impetuous ways. "I can't think why you should be so concerned, Anita," he continued. "Your first duty, I would have thought, is to Miranda."

Abashed by this justified criticism, Anita turned crimson. "I'm sorry, Hugo. You're right, of course. But . . . but Miranda and I were convinced that the . . . viscount . . . Rodney . . . "

"Oh! Never mind that, Hugo," Felix said quickly. "If it hadn't been for Anita, we would never have found the servants in the cellar. I take it you want me to stay here while you go in pursuit of Miranda?" He asked the question deliberately, in order to draw his brother's ire away from Anita.

His ploy was successful, for Lord Romford rounded on him with what amounted to a snarl. "*If* you think you can refrain from tasting the brandy, yes. Otherwise I will ask Jake to spend the night here, for there is no telling what time I shall return."

"I'm not likely to make that mistake again, Hugo," Felix said. "I think I downed enough firewater last night to hold me for quite a while. Anyway, I only acted so foolishly because I was miffed with you."

"Miffed!" Lord Romford exploded, and then, seeing the laughter in his brother's eyes, relaxed slightly. "You're lucky that I have other things to occupy my mind, else I would haul you over the coals for your dreadful behavior of last night. Yes, your help would certainly be appreciated. I dread to think what Miranda is up to, but undoubtedly I will have some kind of mess to contend with when I find her."

"You think she is pursuing Sir Walter to his yacht?" Felix asked, pleased to note that he had succeeded in calming his brother.

Lord Romford nodded. "Or Rodney. I cannot dismiss that possibility."

Anita pressed her lips together, smothering her cry of protest at such a charge. She knew of old that once her cousin was in such a mood he wouldn't listen to any further arguments. Instead, she wiped her hands nervously on her cambric and asked if he wanted them to hold dinner until he returned.

"No, no," Lord Romford replied. "Maybe chef can prepare a cold buffet to await our return, although by the time I have finished with Miranda I'm sure her appetite will have vanished."

"Not Miranda," Felix chuckled. "When she's upset she can't stop eating." The smile left his face as he walked over to his brother, hand extended. "Good luck, Hugo," he said soberly. "I hope you find the chit in one piece."

Lord Romford took Felix's hand and shook it briefly. "Have no worry on that score," he said with an attempt at light-heartedness. "It's the person she's chasing you should have sympathy for. Now, if you'll excuse me, I'd best be off."

Anita followed him out of the room quickly. She could sense that Felix was about to ask her some very awkward questions, and she was not prepared to answer them. "Would you mind if we dined early, Felix?" she asked, pausing at the door. "I would like to be ready just in case Miranda needs help when Hugo brings her home."

"Not at all," Felix responded, genuinely concerned about Anita's pallor. "Why don't you rest until then? It might do you some good. Bring back the color to your cheeks."

Anita put a hand to her face nervously. "I'm ... I'm perfectly all right, Felix. It's ... it's just that Miranda and I can't believe that Rodney ..."

"Say no more," Felix interrupted in kindly tones. "Neither can I, really. But you know Hugo, once he has a bee in his bonnet over something there's no arguing with him."

Anita nodded miserably. "I ... I just hope that Miranda manages to get news of him. It would be too dreadful never to know what has become of him." As she spoke she felt tears well up behind her eyes. "Dinner at six?" she asked in trembling tones, and as soon as Felix nodded, she thankfully fled the room. If she had continued that conversation, she would have confessed everything to Felix and broken her promise to Miranda.

Felix stood where he was for several minutes and then shrugged. "It's easy to see what ails her," he observed, "but that, surely, is one complication we could all do without at this juncture."

Later that evening, just as Anita was beginning to wonder if she could safely pretend she was going to bed, Watkins entered the sitting room.

"Excuse me for bothering you, Master Felix, but there is a messenger from Rossfield wanting to see Lord Romford."

"Show him in," Felix said quickly. "He might have news that cannot wait."

They both recognized the man Watkins ushered in as Humphries and it was apparent that the servant was frightened. Felix, assuming control, rose and greeted him with a smile.

"Humphries!" he exclaimed. "You look troubled. Is there anything I can do?"

Humphries looked at him dubiously. "I dunno about that," he muttered uneasily. "Mr. Wilkins was most particular that I speak with nobody but Lord Romford."

"But that would necessitate a long wait," Felix responded. "He's out and we've no idea when to expect him."

"Lordy me!" Humphries sighed unhappily. "That does make things difficult. Very difficult indeed."

"We can act on behalf of Lord Romford," Anita interposed, instinct telling her that Humphries's news involved the viscount. "I'm sure Mr. Wilkins wouldn't expect you to wait here all night."

"Well . . ." Humphries hesitated. "It's these strange noises that are coming from behind the wood paneling in the dining room. . . ."

"Yes . . ." Anita prompted.

"We . . . we don't know what they is, but . . . but . . . Mr. Wilkins thought Lord Romford should know and . . . and possibly want to investigate." He looked hopefully toward Felix and was rewarded with a nod. A look of relief spread across his weatherbeaten face as he exclaimed, "You mean you don't mind 'aving to return to Rossfield?"

"Not at all," Felix said grandly. "I need three minutes to change out of these confounded clothes and we can be off."

"Make it five," Anita said, hastily scrambling to her feet. "I have no intention of being left behind." She was gone before Felix could protest and returned within four minutes, suitably clad for a night ride.

Once inside Rossfield, Felix did his best to allay any fears the servants had, but it was really Anita's presence that made them less apprehensive. For, as Humphries said later, after Felix had dismissed them, "If a mere woman ain't afraid, then I'm dashed if I knows what there is to be frightened of."

"That's no way to talk about Miss Mayberry," Mr. Wilkins tutted disapprovingly. "But, I agree, her presence is enough to cast a different complexion on the whole matter."

Meanwhile, Felix and Anita, safely ensconced in the dining room, were sitting quietly waiting for the noises to start up again.

"I hope you didn't mind me dismissing Wilkins," Felix was saying. "I thought it a prudent move. I mean, if we do discover something horrendous, we don't want to frighten the servants any more than they have been."

Anita shudded. "I hope that won't be the case," she said in a small voice. "I . . . I don't think I could bear it."

Felix stood up and paced the room restlessly. "If you don't mind, old girl, I think I'll go and see if there's a secret passageway, similar to the one at Ramsden. It's quite obvious to me that if someone is behind one of these walls, there must be an entrance and it's probably outside."

"Please do as you wish," Anita said, "for I must confess that your fidgety ways increase my own nervousness. Only . . . only you will let me know if you discover anything?"

"Naturally. We're in this together, old girl. For I can tell you one thing, if we botch this up and

Hugo finds out, I don't want to face him by myself."

Anita was forced to laugh at this. "Go on, you coward," she urged. "And if I hear any noises, I'll try talking to whoever is there until you return."

Eighteen

Miranda wished she could urge Firefly to go faster, but knew that if she did so, she would run the possibility of winding him.

"Don't worry, Firefly," she encouraged. "We're nearly there and I promise to give you an extra ration of oats when we return."

The exhilaration she felt at having succeeded thus far in her adventure was tremendous, and even this was heightened by the fact that her efforts of deduction had proved to be so masterful.

After Felix and Anita had left the house, she had ridden to the Rose and Crown at Tintern. It would be difficult to explain why, but somehow it had just seemed the obvious place to start looking for the viscount's hunter. And indeed she had not been disappointed, for the horse was there.

However, her discreet inquiries of Phelps had elicited no satisfactory response. Phelps had been quite ready to divulge that a closed chaise had been waiting outside the inn a full hour before a heavily caped man had ridden up. Unfortunately, the man had quickly tied his horse to the hitching post before he stepped into the coach. This had all happened so quickly, no one had recognized him.

"I'm blowed if I know what to make of it, and that's for sure," Phelps had said. "I mean, 'tis a well-known fact that nobody else but 'is lordship can ride that 'orse. But if it were 'im, then I don't see no need for secrecy. 'E's normally friendly and always 'as time to bid me good-day."

"Perhaps he was in a hurry," Miranda suggested helpfully. "If it was Viscount Brynmawr. What direction did you say the coach went?" She posed the question casually and after a moment's hesitation Phelps answered that he rather thought the chaise took off in the direction of Newport.

"In fact it must 'ave, 'cause I remember thinking to myself that maybe as 'ow 'is lordship might be going off to join Sir Walter on 'is yacht."

On hearing this, Miranda had quickly said goodbye and hurried back to Ramsden. Ensuring that Mrs. Branley was still in her room, she changed into the clothes of Felix's she had left on her bed. That, she was forced to admit to herself now, had been a mistake. She should have changed before going to Tintern, risking the possible censure of Phelps, then she wouldn't have bumped into Mrs. Branley, and been forced to endure the tirade that venerable old lady had subjected her to.

Miranda laughed softly as she recalled the look of outrage that had spread across Mrs. Branley's face on seeing her dressed as a boy. But, somehow, she had escaped and had even managed to tell Mrs. Branley to give Hugo the message that she was leaving for Newport in pursuit of the person they had all been looking for. What Hugo would say when he discovered she was missing was something she decided not to worry about, at least for the time being.

And, now, here she was in Newport. Reining Firefly in, she sat looking down at the harbor. Several boats were lying at anchor and she spotted *The Tawny Owl* immediately. It was the only three-masted one there.

"Come on, Firefly," she murmured. "We're almost at the end of our adventure." She trotted down the hill at a brisk pace, humming a sea chanty to herself. A closed chaise was pulling away from the loading area as she arrived and without stopping to think of the consequences, she hailed the driver. Hadn't Phelps said that whoever it had been had driven away from the Rose and Crown in a closed carriage?

Adopting a gruff voice she bid the man good-evening. "Can you tell me who your passenger was?" she asked. "I'm looking for my uncle before he sets sail."

The coachman shrugged his shoulders. "I wouldna' know, laddie. I just brought him from Tintern, like I was paid to."

"Then it may be my uncle," Miranda exclaimed, slapping her thigh, "for that is where we are from. 'Tis a famous thing that I thought to hail you, for now you can tell me which ship he boarded."

The man eyed her suspiciously. "No, you look 'ere, laddie, if's there anything 'avey-cavey about this ride, I'll 'ave to say right now, I'm not involved. I were just doing what I was paid to do, like." His heavy Welsh accent made it difficult for Miranda to understand him and she leaned forward in her saddle to try and catch his words.

"It's nothing like that, mister, it's only that my uncle has forgotten an important letter." She patted her breast pocket earnestly. "My aunt was furious when she discovered it and sent me after him post haste."

"Well . . . " the coachman began, "I think it was that one over there. The one with the blue mast."

Miranda dug deep into her jacket pocket and produced a couple of coins. "Thank you. Thank you," she said, pressing the money into the outstretched hand. "You're very kind."

She watched him drive away and then looked about to see where she could tether Firefly. She felt more than reluctant above leaving him unattended, thereby risking the possibility of having him stolen. She gave an involuntary shudder at the thought. Lord Romford would certainly never forgive her if that happened.

A young boy strolling by caught her attention and she called him over. "I say, what's your name?"

"Tim, mister," the boy said, doffing his cap.

"Do you work here?"

The boy nodded. "On that yacht yonder," he replied, pointing behind him vaguely.

"In that case, would you mind holding my horse awhile? I have to visit a ship and don't want him stolen."

"'Twould be no trouble at all, mister. I'm not due back on board until six bells."

Miranda slid off Firefly and handed the reins over. "Thank you, Tim. I'll make it worth your while when I return."

Knowing that the young boy was looking at her, she swaggered boldly over to Sir Walter's ketch. She could see that preparations were in progress for sailing and smiled grimly. "You will go empty-handed, Sir Walter," she muttered. "For I shall insist on your returning the coins to me."

Without more ado she boarded and stood on the deck waiting for someone to notice her. The atmosphere was one of controlled chaos. Each crew member was busy with his own task. Seeing a sailor winding rope, Miranda stepped over to him and tapped him on the shoulder.

"I say," she commanded impatiently, "can I have a word with you?"

The sailor straightened up slowly, giving her a toothless grin. "Me, mister?" he inquired carelessly. "Now 'ow could the likes of I 'elps the likes of you?"

"I want to see your captain." The man seemed to hesitate, so she added quickly, "Immediately."

"And who might I say it is?" the sailor inquired.

Nonplused for a moment by this unexpected question, Miranda stared at him blankly. "Tell him . . . tell him I have come with a message from the Viscount of Brynmawr."

The man scurried away and as Miranda waited

she looked across the harbor to check on Firefly. She was beginning to feel a little uneasy and wanted to ensure that her only avenue of escape was still there. She gave a little sigh of relief as she picked out the boy still standing where she had left him, but then frowned as she saw him deep in conversation with an older man. They seemed to be discussing something with some urgency. The thought that the boy might be trying to sell Firefly crossed her mind, but she dismissed it quickly. He had struck her as being an honest individual, unlike any of the crew on Sir Walter's ship. The whole bunch looked and acted like barbarians. However, as she continued to look at Tim, she couldn't deny that she felt a lot easier when the man moved away empty-handed.

Suddenly all the noise on the boat died away and her uneasiness increased. She started back to the gangplank she had used to board and noticed, to her alarm, it was no longer in place. She turned in panic and saw, too late, a man standing behind her, his arm raised and in his hand an iron bar. Before she had time to cry out, the man's arm came down, delivering a blow to the side of her head. The last thing she beheld before falling to the ground was the toothless grin of the sailor.

Tim, who had been trying to comply with the order issued by his captain to keep an eye on the events taking place on Sir Walter's yacht, saw the scuffle, but was uncertain as to the outcome. Dusk was closing in rapidly, making it difficult for him to observe. Mindful of the captain's instructions not to leave his post, he called out, with some urgency, for assistance. He knew the captain had returned to *The Tawny Owl*, but the night watchman from the ketch was supposed to be near at hand.

Help, in the end, though, came from a totally unexpected quarter. Lord Romford arrived on the dock in time to hear Tim's cry. He recognized his horse before he did the cabin boy and with a slight jerk of his wrists he brought the phaeton to a standstill. He jumped down with a grace that belied his size, and greeted Tim by asking him what he was doing with Firefly.

"I dunno m'lord," Tim replied, bowing deeply in respect. "A young man asked me to mind 'im and then Captain Jones comes along and says it's one of yours and I'm not to move."

Lord Romford eyed him thoughtfully as he tried to make sense of this piece of information. "The young man, where did he go?"

"He boarded Sir Walter's ship, m'lord. I . . . I told Captain Jones and 'e didn't know whether to follow 'im or wait to see what developed."

"And what caused you to call out, Tim?"

Tim scratched his head in bewilderment. "I was trying to keep an eye on things, but what with the failing light and all the activity going on, I don't know. Only it seems to me that the young man was 'it on the 'ead."

Lord Romford let out an oath. His deep concern over Miranda's safety chased away his anger. "Fetch Captain Jones," he commanded. "I'll take Firefly."

"Yes, sir . . . m'lord," Tim replied and made off at the double.

While he waited for Captain Jones, Lord Romford tied the horse to the back of his carriage, all the while chiding himself for not considering the danger Miranda was putting herself in. As he had driven at a recklessly fast pace from Tintern he had been consumed with anger and had given much thought to the various punishments he would mete out to his ward when he caught up with her. All of them, in some way, entailed being under his watchful eye. None of them allowing her the freedom it seemed she craved. Now, nothing mattered except her safety.

"Aha! My lord," Captain Jones said. "I'm glad you arrived. I was concerned about young Felix but didn't know what to do."

"Felix!" Lord Romford exclaimed. "'Tis not Felix aboard that ship, but my ward."

Captain Jones, unable to contain the astonishment he felt, stared at Lord Romford in horror. "If I'd only known," he breathed. "I would have followed her immediately. I just assumed it was Felix from Tim's description."

Lord Romford gave a hollow laugh. "Come, Captain, it's still not too late. We have time to board. They have yet to hoist their sails."

The captain turned and said something to Tim who was just behind him. "Tell Albert and Adam to follow us, Tim, and tell them to arm themselves."

For the second time, Tim ran off and Lord Romford strode toward Sir Walter's ship. "At least they haven't cast off yet," he said. "I'll jump on first, Captain Jones." Without waiting for an answer, he waited for the swell to abate before taking the leap from the dock to the boat. As he landed, a sailor ran up to him and demanded to know what he was doing.

"I have business with your captain," Lord Romford said tersely. "Inform him that

Lord Romford wishes to speak with him."

The sailor stared rudely before walking off slowly. And as Lord Romford waited, he found his interest mounting, despite his concern for Miranda's welfare, to see who would obey the summons. Sir Walter or the viscount.

Nineteen

It seemed to Anita that hours had elapsed since she had started her lonely vigil. She had begun tapping a few panels, hoping to hear a telltale hollow sound, but the enormity of the task was daunting. The entire room was paneled from floor to ceiling.

"It would take me two days, and I'd still be here," she told herself angrily. However, refusing to be downcast, she dragged a dining chair to one wall and systematically began to tap it with one hand, using the other to feel the ornate carving for some type of lever.

Then, suddenly, she heard a strange noise coming from the other side of the room. It sounded like a moan. It was followed by another and then another. Jumping down from the chair, she ran across the threadbare carpet and started to call out reassurances. She looked around wildly, hoping to see a latch, anything that would open the secret door, but once again was unsuccessful. After a few minutes of fruitless searching she sank down on her knees in despair. Pressing her fingers to her temples in an effort to ease the pain in her head, she forced herself to think of what to do next.

"I have it," she exclaimed jubilantly and stood up, an excited gleam in her eyes. "Listen carefully, please," she said loudly to the wall. "I know it's you, Rodney, and I need your help to free you. You are to knock once if the answers to my questions are yes, twice if they are no." She paused briefly and then asked, "Do you understand, my darling?"

There was silence, and then she heard a faint tap. Clapping her hands exultantly, she gave a small pirouette. "Do you know how I can free you?" she asked and experienced a moment of anxiety before she heard a single knock. Buoyed by her success she worked patiently in response to the answers she received and finally located the lever. Quickly depressing it, she stood to one side as a panel slid back revealing a priest's hole. There, bound and gagged, was the viscount.

"My darling, my darling," she cried, her pleasure at finding her alive causing her to forget all modesty. "I'll have you free in a minute." Her fingers were trembling so, she had difficulty with the knot of the gag, but eventually loosened it sufficiently to move it down.

"Thalassa!" she murmured, slipping the gag over the viscount's chin. "Thalassa!"

The viscount's gaze had not wavered from Anita's face and once he was free he was unable to do more than look at her in speechless wonder.

"My dearest angel," he said, pursing his lips to bring some life to them. "My darling Anita."

His voice sounded thick and the ugly line about his mouth made Anita wince. The gag had been so tight, it would be a long time before the bruise disappeared. She brought her hand up slowly and gently massaged the mark, until the opening of the door drew her attention.

"Oh! . . . Oh! . . . Felix," she said breathlessly. "It's . . . it's . . . Rodney. I've found him."

"So I observe," Felix said, an eyebrow raised at the compromising position the two of them were in. "So I observe."

"Felix," the viscount began, his mouth twitching in pain, "get me out of these bonds and I'll explain everything later." He gave Anita a smile of reassurance and whispered, "The need for secrecy is over, my little one."

"Please hurry, Felix," Anita begged, remaining where she was. "You can see how tightly Rodney had been bound by looking at the marks on his face. A knife is needed, for I can tell you the knots are impossible to untie."

Felix stood looking at her with a bemused expression. Until this very moment he hadn't realized how pretty she was. Now, her face aglow with happiness, she looked positively beautiful. "Yes . . . yes," he said at length. "Of course." He dipped his hand into his pocket and retrieved a small silver object. He gave it an expert flick with his thumb and a blade emerged. "I'm afraid I'm going to have to ask you to move, Anita," he continued, and Anita, realizing for the first time the wanton picture she presented, sprang up hastily.

The viscount sank back onto his side, presenting his bound limbs to Felix. "Try not to cut my jacket," he said, "for Walter has disposed of all my clothes in an effort to support his story that I had left for Europe."

Felix grunted as he started to cut through the rope, "I'll be as careful as I can," and continued to work in silence until the last bond fell in shreds to the floor.

The viscount lay still for a few minutes until Anita, who could bear it no longer, came to him and started to rub some life back into his arms and hands. "My poor darling," she soothed as she saw him press his lips together in pain. "I'll try not to hurt you."

Felix, taking his cue from Anita's actions, bent over and began to massage the viscount's feet.

"In any other instance," the viscount said, attempting to make light of his painful condition, "I would've enjoyed this, but the thought that my dear nephew left me in this hole to die quite takes the pleasure out of your ministrations."

Anita let go of his hand briefly to put a finger over his lips. "Ssssh, my darling. I cannot bear to contemplate such a terrible fate." The viscount grinned but did as he was bid. "Try clenching your fist," Anita said, doing her best to ignore the wild beating of her heart. "There, does that feel a little better? And your feet, are they coming back to life?"

Felix paused in his work to look at the couple in front of him. Unable to contain his curiosity any longer he grabbed one of the viscount's feet firmly and said, "I refuse to continue aiding you, Rodney, unless you tell me what lies between you and Anita."

Anita looked at the viscount nervously but, emboldened by his smile of encouragement, relaxed.

"It was never my desire to conceal my feelings for Anita," he said with touching simplicity, "but Miranda . . ."

"Miranda!" Felix exclaimed. "And all this time I was worrying about how to break the news to her of your double dealing! I should have known she'd be behind the whole thing."

"It's all become such a muddle really," Anita said, "that I, quite honestly, am confused as to how we let Miranda talk us into anything."

"There's no need for explanations," Felix sympathized. "I'm sure she had her reasons. However, Rodney, what concerns me more at the moment is the whereabouts of Walter."

"I suspect he is on his way to France, with the coins that belong to your family."

"We knew it was either you or Walter who had taken them," Felix said, "although neither Hugo nor I could really bring ourselves to believe that you were involved . . . only . . . only Walter had quite a convincing tale to tell this morning."

"I'm sure," the viscount said grimly, "making me out to be the blackguard he really is."

"Well, none of us believed it," Anita declared, "and I knew you to be in danger."

The viscount took her hand in his and caressed it slowly. "Thank you, my love," he whispered. "I knew you would stand by me, no matter what anyone said. That is what sustained me these last twenty-four hours. It was almost as though I could sense your belief."

"Oh! Rodney," Anita cried. "I would have died if anything had happened to you."

Obviously embarrassed by this open display of emotion, Felix stood up and coughed discreetly. "I hate to interrupt," he said, "but I think it only fair you tell us what happened. After all, we have all of us at some point nearly risked our necks trying to get to the bottom of this little mystery. Even now, Miranda and Hugo are probably engaged in some terrifying duel at the docks in Newport."

"What!" the viscount shouted, struggling to stand. "We must follow immediately. Walter is a desperate man and will stop at nothing to accomplish his aim."

Anita tried to calm him, but he shook her off. "No, my darling, I must go."

"You'll have to fight me first, old boy," Felix drawled in a good imitation of his brother's voice. "If I know Hugo, he is almost home by now. They've been gone for hours."

"And if they don't return?" the viscount asked. "I'm telling you, Felix, Walter is capable of the worst sort of behavior."

"And so is Hugo, if events dictate it," Felix reassured. "Anyway, he is not without protection in the harbor, for his own boat is moored there. Why don't you sit down and tell us the truth?"

The viscount shook his head in defeat and hobbled to a chair, leaning on Anita's shoulder for support. "On one condition, Felix," he said, "and that is if we don't hear from Hugo in an hour, we go to Newport."

"Agreed. Now, make yourself comfortable and I'll pour you a drink."

The viscount accepted this offer gratefully.

"Are you hungry, my dearest?" Anita asked. "You cannot have eaten in an age. Let me ring for Wilkins and see what he can find."

"Oh! Lord," the viscount exclaimed. "I had

forgotten all about the servants. Are they all right?"

"We found them in the cellar in mint condition," Anita smiled. "Humphries complained a little because of the uncomfortable night he had spent, but Fred and Wilkins seemed to take it all in their stride. Shall I ring for them?"

"No, no, not just yet. Let me tell you what happened before Felix loses all patience with me."

"Did you know Anthony Roberts?" Anita asked timidly, anxious to clear up that part of the story first. "It seems that Walter claimed you were in collusion with him."

"Walter would say anything to save his own skin. Yes, I knew Roberts. I knew him because he was trying to blackmail me."

"So you did meet with him the night before he was killed?" Felix asked.

The viscount nodded. "I rather hoped that that fact had escaped everyone's notice. Indeed, I had another appointment with him the following day, but he died before he could keep it. You see, he and Walter were working together, stealing pictures from Hugo and replacing them with reproductions. Very good ones, I might add. Then, unfortunately for Roberts, on one of his nocturnal visits to Ramsden, via the secret passage, he found the ring."

"He knew the significance of it?" Felix asked in astonishment.

"As a local man he had heard the legend of the coins," the viscount replied. "Anyway, he showed the trinket to Walter, who naturally was delighted and encouraged him to find the coins."

"But how could he?" Felix interjected. "It took

us an age and a great deal of luck before Miranda finally came up with the solution."

The viscount shrugged his shoulders. "I don't know, but he did. He told me it took him weeks, but don't forget he found a clue inside the ring. But, be that as it may, having found the hiding place, he then decided to play Walter along for a larger share of the proceeds."

"Silly man," Anita said. "He must have known he was signing his own death warrant. I can't imagine Walter agreeing to such a scheme."

"Of course not, my dearest, but Roberts expected Walter's refusal and contacted me, demanding a thousand guineas for his silence. Far more than he knew he would get from Walter."

"And if you didn't comply?" Felix asked.

"He would expose Walter as the thief he was and create a great scandal for our family name."

"My poor darling," Anita said. "What a dreadful position to put you in. Were you going to pay him?"

"I was prepared to give him something, if it became necessary, but my primary concern was to buy back the pictures and restore them before Hugo discovered they were missing."

"A bit risky, don't you think?" Felix said. "Hugo knew an age ago, which is why he suspected you when you failed to tell him."

"Oh! Don't think I wasn't tempted to confide in him, but I wanted to keep the scandal within the family. On reflection, though, you're right, Felix. My actions must have appeared most peculiar for an innocent man."

"Odd, I agree," Felix said, "but you had the ladies' support."

"I hope you will never find your faith in me to

be misplaced," the viscount said quietly to Anita.

She smiled at him, tears misting her eyes. "It wasn't difficult for me to believe in your innocence, for I knew you to be totally incapable of such fiendish behavior. Also, I had an advantage over Hugo and Felix. I knew you would never have proposed marriage if you had been guilty."

"Wait until I get my hands on Miranda," Felix laughed. "The scheming little minx knew all of this and never uttered a word."

"Out of loyalty to me," Anita interjected. "And . . . and I think she was looking forward to proving to Hugo how remiss he had been in his judgment of Rodney."

"Well . . . " Felix started thoughtfully, "if I'm not mistaken, she can spend the rest of her life telling him."

The viscount looked at Felix in surprise. "Whatever do you mean?"

"It's only guesswork, of course, but wouldn't you agree that when two such volatile people are at each other's throats constantly, it's a sure indication they're in love?"

"The trouble is, Felix," Anita said, "I don't think either of them realizes it yet."

Twenty

Lord Romford pulled out his watch impatiently and noted that he had been kept waiting for a full five minutes. Certainly long enough for the crew to hide Miranda.

"The captain must be playing for time," Captain Jones said. "But if he thinks he can get past *The Tawny Owl* and out to sea, he'll have to think again."

"You may be right, Captain. However, my concern, for the moment, is my ward's safety. Tim thinks he saw her being hit on the head."

Captain Jones grunted, not quite knowing what to say. He had never seen his master so perturbed.

Swearing to himself, Lord Romford started for the bridge, determined to put an end to the charade. "Stay put, Captain," he said, "while I try to settle this once and for all."

The nasal twang of a familiar voice halted him before he had taken more than a few steps. "My dear Hugo, I'm so terribly sorry to have kept you waiting."

Lord Romford looked up toward the bridge and curled his lip before replying coldly, "I should have known that you were the one, Walter. Rodney would never stoop so low."

Sir Walter laughed and tossed his head back in what struck Lord Romford as an entirely feminine gesture. "Unfortunately, Hugo," he drawled, "Rodney would rather remain poor than take the necessary risks to become a wealthy man."

"I haven't come here to discuss Rodney," Lord Romford said icily. "Merely to reclaim my property."

"Aha! The coins, no doubt. I'm afraid I no longer have them in my possession."

"No, Walter, not the coins. Someone far more important," he said, emphasizing the word someone. "My ward."

"Miranda?" Sir Walter said. "I'm afraid you are mistaken. I most certainly do not have her."

Angered by Sir Walter's calm and obvious lie, Lord Romford quickly climbed the steps to the bridge. "I have no intention of discussing this subject in public," he said waving a hand to the sailors who were staring at him agape with curiosity. "I would suggest you take me to your cabin where we can discuss this matter in private." He moved a step closer, forcing Sir Walter to drop back a pace.

"My dear fellow, there's no need to be so heated. Has it not occurred to you that Miranda might have run off with Rodney? Really," he continued brushing his sleeve absentmindedly, "I refuse to be held responsible for her disappearance."

Lord Romford steadied himself against a handrail as the ship rode a wave awkwardly. "Enough of that kind of talk," he said curtly, trying to control the urge to hit Sir Walter squarely on the jaw, "or you will live to regret it. Now, let us go below before I lose my temper."

Sir Walter, evidently realizing that it would behoove him to comply with the suggestion, turned to a man standing behind him and ordered him to take command. "And, Mr. Richards," he added softly, "if I'm not back on deck in ten minutes you know what to do." He turned abruptly and led the way to his cabin.

"My patience is at an end with you, Walter," Lord Romford cautioned as soon as they were alone. "So, I warn you not to fob me off with any more of your lies. I want Miranda and I refuse to leave this ship without her."

Sir Walter shrugged his shoulders and was about to say something before apparently changing his mind. Instead, he stood there, a supercilious expression on his face.

"I know of your involvement with the man, Anthony Roberts, and if you continue to deny that you have Miranda prisoner, I, personally, will see to it that charges of murder are brought against you."

"Hugo, Hugo," Sir Walter said softly. "What makes you think you will leave this ship alive?"

"My captain and the crew of *The Tawny Owl* will ensure that, you fool," Lord Romford replied. "Do not think you can intimidate me with empty threats. You might have succeeded in frightening

Rodney, but, I beg you, do not underestimate me. I will kill you without a moment's hesitation if you don't restore Miranda to me immediately."

"I see," Sir Walter said with great deliberation. "You seem so very certain that she is on board."

"She was seen, you fool," Lord Romford snapped.

"It would appear that my luck has run out," Sir Walter murmured. "And, if I do as you ask?"

"As far as I'm concerned, you are free to leave port," Lord Romford replied, thankful that Sir Walter was at last displaying some sense. "And, if you value your life, I would suggest that you never set foot in England again."

Sir Walter shook his head thoughtfully. "You drive a hard bargain, Hugo. A very hard bargain. But"—again he shrugged his shoulders—"you leave me no choice." He rang a small hand bell and the cabin door opened immediately. "Mr. Stevens, be so good as to bring up the young lad we have in the hold." Mr. Stevens nodded and left without a word. "As you can see, Hugo, I too am not without protection. Do I have your word that I will not be hounded by anyone?"

"You credit yourself with too much importance," Lord Romford replied. For the first time since he had boarded, he relaxed slightly. Even so, he knew he wouldn't be completely at ease until he had Miranda safely on shore. "I cannot think of one person who would want to pursue you." He broke off as the door opened. He let out an oath as he saw Mr. Stevens drag in the inert body of Miranda. "You heathen," he exploded. "What have you done?"

"I'm afraid one of my men got carried away,

but she will be all right. A little stunned, nothing more. Thank you, Mr. Stevens, you may go."

Lord Romford strode over to his ward's side and dropped to one knee to examine her. As he did so, Miranda opened one eye and gave him a brave little smile.

"Oh! Hugo," she breathed. "I never thought to see a friendly face again. Thank goodness you are here."

He scanned her face quickly for signs of stress. Then, satisfied that other than the blow to her head she was unharmed, he helped her to a sitting position. He was aware of his heart pounding and almost gave way to a strange desire to hold her close. Indeed, he would have done so had Sir Walter not been watching them. It took all his self-control to stand up and turn his back on her.

Miranda shook her head and gingerly touched the bruise on her temple. "Can . . . can we go, Hugo?" she asked tentatively. "I'm . . . I'm sorry to have caused you so much trouble, but . . . but I thought to be able to force Walter to tell me what he had done with Rodney and the coins."

Lord Romford turned quickly at this, for Miranda's words forced him to recall her engagement to the viscount. Fool that he was, he had erased that fact from his mind. No wonder Miranda had ridden posthaste after Sir Walter. He felt a great pain in his chest and abruptly turned away again. He could not bear to see her looking so forlorn.

Miranda was completely unnerved by Lord Romford's silence. Misunderstanding his cool attitude, which she thought to be directed at herself, she wondered if he would ever forgive her foolish behavior. Sighing unhappily, she rose and stood, swaying slightly until she was able to stay the trembling in her legs.

"Very touching," Sir Walter observed cynically. "A highly competent performance, Miranda. Did you really believe you could force me to reveal anything to you? I would have enjoyed teaching you a lesson for all the trouble you have caused me. Had it not been for you, nobody would have known about Roberts." He took a step forward but found his way blocked by Lord Romford.

"I wouldn't try anything silly, Walter," Lord Romford said very softly. "Just tell me what you have done with Rodney and we'll be on our way."

"Rodney, my dear fellow, is languishing in the priest's hole at Rossfield. The one in the dining room." He pulled out his watch and after a few minutes of calculation continued, "I would think that if you returned there quickly, you might be in time to save him. Though why I tell you this is beyond me, for it matters not to me if Rodney is alive or dead."

"I always knew you to be a despicable cad," Miranda said, a look of loathing on her face. "How could you do such a thing to your own flesh and blood?"

Sir Walter gave an unpleasant laugh. "You poor little rich girl," he said, his lip curling sarcastically. "You will never know what it means to be penniless. You will never experience hunger or deprivation. So don't even try to judge me. You, who sit in your gold-lined tower, will never know to what ends a man such as I will go to satisfy his need for money. . . ." He broke off and sank into a chair, a look of defeat on his face.

"Go . . . go . . . " he started, but his voice was trembling too much for him to continue.

Lord Romford looked at him contemptuously, then took Miranda by the arm and silently led her away. He could feel her shaking and once again had to resist the temptation to hold her close. He would have dearly loved to have dealt properly with Sir Walter but had to satisfy himself that exile was punishment enough.

"Come along, Miranda," he said instead, his tone cool. "We have no time to waste."

Miranda nodded, too numbed by his harsh voice to speak. She longed for some words of reassurance but could tell by his expression that they wouldn't come from him.

"I'll leave Firefly with Captain Jones," he continued brusquely. "Tim can ride him over to Ramsden on the morrow."

Once on deck he greeted Captain Jones with the news that Sir Walter was to be allowed to sail and within minutes of leaving the ship he swung Miranda into his phaeton and set off for Rossfield at a fast pace.

Not a word was spoken on the journey. Miranda, unable to control the misery she felt, sniffed back the tears. Several times she stole a look at her guardian's stern profile hoping for some indication that he had forgiven her. But his eyes remained on the road ahead, his brow creased by a frown.

"It's hopeless," she muttered to herself. "Absolutely hopeless. I'll never be able to call him my friend again." However, the wind took her words and carried them away and her unhappiness increased.

At long last she recognized the steeple of Itton

Church and she sent up a thankful prayer. She
was glad the journey was nearly over, though
quite what she would do when they finally
reached Ramsden she didn't know. One thing was
clear, and that was she couldn't stay there.
Nothing could be as bad as having to endure the
lasting displeasure of her guardian. She would
announce her intention of returning to London in
the morning and endeavor to find something to do
that would occupy her mind and help her forget.

"We're here," Lord Romford said curtly, jumping down. "I hope we're in time."

Miranda scrambled down, not waiting to be
helped, and followed Lord Romford to the front
door. He tugged the bell viciously, refusing to
look down at his ward. If the truth were to be
told, he didn't dare. He did not trust himself to
say the right thing to allay her fears about the
viscount's safety.

The doors were flung open and Lord Romford
brushed past Mr. Wilkins.

"Good evening, m'lord," Mr. Wilkins said, a
look of relief spreading across his face. "I'm so
very glad you are here. Master Felix and Miss
Mayberry are already in the dining room."

Surprised by this, Lord Romford paused
momentarily, as though to seek an explanation,
but deciding that enough time had been wasted,
merely thanked him for the information and
strode toward the dining room.

He opened the doors and stopped at the
threshold, a look of fury crossing his face. Miranda, who was right behind him, tried to pass him
but found her way firmly blocked.

"Hugo," she urged, "quickly, before it is too
late." Nothing in her bearing betrayed her inward

misgivings, but Lord Romford's reaction to the scene beyond frightened her. It was obvious they were, indeed, too late.

"I'll deal with this," Lord Romford said in a strangled voice. "You stay here, Miranda." He advanced into the room and stood, arms akimbo, as Anita detached herself from the viscount's embrace. "I hope you can explain yourself, Rodney," he began tersely but stopped as Miranda pushed past him and ran to the viscount's side.

"Oh! Rodney," she cried, tears of relief streaming down her cheeks, "I'm so glad you are safe. I was so afraid we wouldn't get here in time." She turned and saw Anita and smiled mistily. "And you, dear Anita, is all well with you?"

Lord Romford, goaded beyond endurance at the viscount's blatant display of affection for another woman, put his hand to his sword menacingly. "It would seem, Miranda, that in your absence he has been quick to find solace with another. I'll ask you again, Rodney, to explain your actions."

"Hold on there, Hugo," Felix interrupted. He knew his brother's moods well, but even he had never seen him in such a towering passion. "Rodney is still recovering from near suffocation."

"In the arms of Anita? Such perfidiousness is not something I take lightly."

"What ever is the matter?" Miranda asked, her amazement at Lord Romford's attitude causing her to forget her own unhappiness. "Are you not pleased to see Rodney alive?"

Lord Romford rounded on her, wishing there was a way he could break the news of her fiancé's unfaithfulness gently. "My concern, at this very moment, is for your ultimate happiness, Miranda and ... and ... I do not think it lies with Rodney. I'm afraid that I cannot allow you to marry him. He is not worthy of you."

"Rodney? Not worthy?" Miranda repeated. "But, I have no intention of marrying him." Too late she realized she had spoken without thinking. "Oh! Anita. Rodney! Can you forgive me?" She faced her guardian squarely and was pleased to note that he looked totally bewildered.

He shook his head slowly, several times, and asked in such a low voice that only she could hear. "You knew? And you don't mind?"

There was an unmistakable caress in his tone that sent a shiver down her spine. "I knew of it days ago," she whispered breathlessly, "but thought it a secret best kept."

"Why, you little minx," he replied, looking down at her adoringly. "I have spent an age wondering how I could break up your engagement."

"I thought it was what you wanted for me, Hugo," she responded mischievously. "And ... and for once I was determined to please you."

He stepped closer to her, oblivious to everything except his pounding heart. "There is only one way you can please me," he said hoarsely, "and that is to become my wife."

Miranda gasped as he gathered her into his arms and kissed her ruthlessly. "Hugo, Hugo," she murmured faintly, "I thought you would never ask."

Anita's discreet cough interrupted any further exchange and they broke apart reluctantly.

"It would seem as though congratulations are

to be offered all round, just as I predicted," Felix said, stepping forward. "Though why it took you such an age to discover what I've known for the longest time, my dear brother, I'll never know."

"You did?" Lord Romford asked, drawing Miranda into the shelter of his arms. "And, to think, I have always thought you to be without a whit of sense."

About the author:

Leonora Blythe was born in South Wales and moved to the United States in search of adventure ten years ago. Her adventure turned out to be a husband and twin boys now two years old. Always fascinated by the romance of the Regency period, she began writing books of that genre three years ago, using her knowledge of her homeland together with extensive research and lively imagination. She returns frequently to England and Wales to check the accuracy of her work. She believes the popularity of the eighteenth century romance springs from the subconscious rejection by many readers of brash, modern values and an appreciation of the old-fashioned virtues. She is working on her sixth Regency romance, and sees no diminution in the demand for books that allow the reader to escape from the bustle of contemporary life into a more leisurely, mannered age.